The Hide

The Hide

BARRY UNSWORTH

W. W. NORTON & COMPANY• NEW YORK • LONDON

Library of Congress Cataloging-in-Publication Data
Unsworth, Barry, 1930–
    The hide / Barry Unsworth.
        p.   cm.
        ISBN 0-393-03955-2
    I.   Title.
PR6071.N8H53   1996
823'.914—dc20   96-1915 CIP

W.W. Norton & Company, Inc., 500 Fifth Avenue, New York, NY 10110
W.W. Norton & Company Ltd., 10 Coptic Street, London WC1A 1PU

1 2 3 4 5 6 7 8 9 0

Josh . . .

THERE IS REASONS for wanting to get off this stall. Not that I been here long. I only been here a month. Mortimer has been here longer, that's my friend. He's been here since before Easter. A change is as good as a rest, I tell him. He likes it though. There is plenty other jobs, I tell him, this time a year, plenty, but he don't want to move.

It is Mrs Morris mainly. She never lets you alone. Besides, the job is *boring*. Crowds of people going backwards and forwards, the hoopla opposite with that Cyp yelling his head off and if you don't want to look at that and Christ I would not blame you, there is the sea, you can look between the stalls at the sea. I got no time for the sea, myself. A course, I know it gives us fish, which is a brain food. A bloke told me once they are going to farm the ocean bed, actually getting ready to do it, but he was having me on. You will never get men to spend their working lives under water, never.

Old Mrs Morris—she is on at you all the time. *Look at him working that rock,* she says, every five minutes or so, meaning the Cyp. *That's what I call grafting,* she says. She has got hairs growing out of her face, which is continuously wobbling like. She can not keep her head still. *Look,* she says. *Look at him.* I have to look. (Mortimer wouldn't, a course, not Mortimer.) This Cyp has got sticks of rock bunched up in his hand and he is poking away with them, jabbing away with them and yelling, yelling, same thing over and over, *come on—who's having a go— six rings a tanner—any score gets you a prize and a stick a rock—*

stick a rock—stick a genuine Blackpool rock. I can see the shine
on his face from here and his big mouth open all the time, he
goes on yelling even if he happens to be eating a sandwich, that
is disgusting in my opinion. *I got no desire to see the contents of
your mouth, you bloody Cyp.* That is what Mortimer shouted
across to him once, but I dunno if he heard. *That's what I call
grafting,* Mrs Morris says. *Getting the rock in, gives people that
holiday feeling like.* Calls himself Henry but he is a Cyp.
Mortimer says they ought to be kept in compounds, either that
or incarcerated. (He has a big vocabulary, Mortimer not the
Cyp.) Coming in here, taking the bread out of our mouths.
(I often enough seen bread in *his.*) I never knew, before
Mortimer and me had a conversation about it. I mean, I never
liked Henry's eating habits and so on, but Mortimer said you
have to be a realist, they are all the same, they are scum.
Coming in here, taking the bread out of our mouths. *Think
big I always say,* Mrs Morris says.

You can not get away from Mrs Morris on this job. Two
sides to the stall and where they meet is kind of a little glass
cage with her inside it, so she can see both ways, who is fiddling,
who is taking time off. Six attendants to watch, all of them
scum to her. Her cash box in front of her, full a coppers and
tanners and threepenny bits. *That is what I call grafting,* she
says. *You lot*—Her head never stops moving, I'd put an end to
myself. She's got her eye on me now, I got to start shouting.
*You hit the bull you get your picture took. Six shots a shilling,
twopence a time, the camera can't tell no lie.* Over the heads of
the crowd. I never look anybody in the eye on this job. I feel a
fool as a matter a fact. And that is the main reason I want to
get off this stall. I am not suited to it, shouting, making a show
of yourself.

I can hear Mortimer talking next to me but I don't look
round. He has picked somebody out of the crowd, he can do
that, just pick somebody out of the crowd like he'd actually
lifted him over. *Hey, you sir, excuse me sir, yes you, one moment
please.* And the bloke stops and listens. That's another thing

that gets me down here, the noise. All the people on the stalls around, shouting the odds, people screaming on the Dipper and the swings, the Dodgems crashing, the music full blast on the roundabout, O Donna Clara, the crack of the rifles. *Excuse me, sir.* Mortimer has this quiet way of talking but as if he didn't really care, and that is a funny thing, it doesn't matter how much noise there is I can always hear him talking. *Yes. Now you see this target here, the centre button controls a camera, what happens is this, if you hit the bull's eye, that light there, yes, over the target, that light goes on and your photograph is taken. Holding the rifle. Six shots a shilling sir, have a bob's worth, yourself actually holding the rifle, yes. . . . Show the missis, show your mates, well I mean, it's proof, isn't it?* They nearly always have a go when they listen this far, Mortimer has a way with him, very persuasive, besides he is educated, Mortimer is, you can tell. It gives people confidence.

Albert starts up on the other side of me. That's another thing that is getting on my nerves, Albert. He's not a bad bloke but he can only talk about this one thing, this girl he got in the family way when he was a nightwatchman. That is his only topic of conversation. It is limited, Albert, Mortimer once said to him, as a topic of conversation it is limited. The other thing is that he is cross-eyed, so you never know if he is looking at you or what he is feeling. Well, he says, it was dark like. How was I to know? Every night around nine she come and she'd sit talking. Lipstick and all, earrings, silk stockings. She didn't get on with her dad, that's what she'd talk about mostly. Her brother's in the army, he'll be looking for me now, well, bugger him . . . . He ought to have had Plastic Surgery for them eyes, too late now a course, it's gone too far.

Mortimer is standing, watching the man shoot. Mortimer is tall and well-built. He looks like Prince Philip but his nose is shorter. Distinguished, that is the word that springs to mind. He always looks superior. I am the only one on the stall he has any time for, he told me that himself. That is because I am not a typical stall attendant. (His own words.) He always calls me by my full name, Josiah. He is the only reason I would have for not leaving. But what I think is, I could get a different sort of job, I don't have to leave town, me and Mortimer could go on seeing each other. If he wanted to, a course. *That is what I call grafting*, Mrs Morris says and then straight after she belches. She's got no manners at all, she'd never dream of saying pardon or putting her hand up. . . . I take a squint up at the sun. Getting on for four o'clock. It will be time for my break.

'What time is it, Albert?'

'How was I to know, the light wasn't good, man to man, it's quarter past four mate, she always come at night. I never saw her face clear like, not in two bloody months, you don't look at the mantelpiece when you're poking the fire, do you. *Come on now, have a go, you will get somethink better than prizes here.* I'm cold, she says, its cold, she says. Have my jacket, love. It must be warmer in that tent of yours, she says. *Here, you sir, can I have a word?* Earrings, made up like that, I never knew, see, I never knew how old she was, she was only fourteen.'

'Quarter past four, that's past my break-time.'

'Every night I had her down inside the tent, every night for a bloody month I screwed her, wouldn't you of done?'

It must of been too dark for her to see Albert's cross eyes. I wish it could of been me instead of him getting her down inside the tent. I am nearly twenty years old and I never had it yet, not the complete thing. I have had everything but, a course. . . .

I look down the stall at Mrs Morris. 'It is my break-time,' I say. 'I'll be going off for my break.'

'You should of been coming back by now,' she says. She knows I haven't got no watch. I can tell just by looking at her dozy old head that she is going to do me out of my break and I get this feeling coming over me same as I always do when someone is doing me down and I can't do nothing about it, my face gets hot and for a bit I don't see so well, then I hear Mortimer's voice saying, 'Better late than never, my old darling. Quarter past, that's my break-time, so the two of us can go together.' And he don't even wait for an answer, he strips off the white jacket and reaches behind him for his own. Then he just steps over the front of the stall. 'Come on,' he says, 'Josiah, you *slowcoach.*'

'All right,' Mrs Morris says. 'You better both go together, it's a slack time.' But he does not even look at her. Mortimer will never be beholden to nobody. When I first met him, when we first got talking, I asked him what his birthday was and I was not surprised when he said August the twelfth. He is a typical Leo. I am an Aquarian myself.

I do not look at Mrs Morris again either. I put on my jacket, dark brown corduroy, I always wear this with my blue denim shirt, it's a good combination for me because I have blue eyes and dark hair. Mortimer has on his black serge suit, he wears black or navy and always plain ties, maroon, dark blue, mustard, and single colour socks, there is never a stripe or a dot about Mortimer.

He puts his arm round my shoulder as we walk off. Mortimer is six inches taller than me. 'You don't want to let that old bag lay the law down to you,' he says. 'Tell her to get stuffed.' Mortimer is very outspoken, a course. I know he is pleased with me at the moment because of that way he put his arm round my shoulder, but I don't know the reason, he isn't like that all the time. What it is, I'm sensitive to people's feelings. I am psychic, really. So I know I done the right thing. Right for Mortimer and me together, that is, not right for me on my own because I should of stood up to Mrs Morris, but them kind of thoughts mix me up. I think it is more important that Mortimer is pleased with me. I can feel his hand heavy on my shoulder. When we are walking together like this I often get a feeling that I don't weigh nothing and my feet are not taking any weight, but Mortimer's steps are taking us along like. I used to feel the same when I was walking beside my dad. (When I was little I mean, a course, that was before he left us and took up with his own half-sister, my Aunt Sady.)

'These old bags, they need watching,' Mortimer says. 'Where's Mr Morris, anyway?'

'I dunno,' I tell him. 'I never saw no Mr Morris.'

'She did him in.'

'Did she honest?' I think maybe that is why she has the trembles now.

'Ah, bugger it,' he says. 'I don't know. You take everything for gospel. I wouldn't put it past her, though, would you?'

'No.'

'How would you fancy having it with her?'

'Christ, no.'

'You wouldn't get a hard on, not in a thousand years.'

'No.'

'Youth at the prow and pleasure at the helm,' he says. Then he starts smiling. 'You'd be immobilised, Josiah,' he says. He is in a good mood and I feel good too, because we are taking our break together and I will have a chance to get in a bit of conversation with him.

The cafeteria is never very crowded this time of day. I look round as we go in. A couple a lads off the Dodgems, some other blokes I know by sight off the stalls. All the rest the public. We get our tea and carry it over to one of the tables.

I hold my cup in both hands and look over it at Mortimer, thinking now I am going to tell him how I feel about this job, now I am going to get a bit of advice like. He always listens to me, he's the only one ever took any real interest. Mortimer listens, then he says it back to me, only better expressed like, more exact. That might sound funny, but Mortimer has a bigger vocabulary than me. Sometimes when he says things I get a shock, I can't hardly believe them things started out in my own mind. Like when I told him about the Cyp Henry getting me down and it turned out in the course of our conversation that it was the same with all of them. Now I know they should be incarcerated.

That was the time we had our one and only row, because he referred to me as a Gyppo. Not that he meant any harm,

but nobody calls me that. I was born in a house. My dad
settled down. Him and his half-sister and my mother, they
settled down in Nottingham and he went into the carting
business. I was born after that. Not that we got anything in
common, my dad and me, he took up with his own half-sister
and made my mother do all the work. I never go there now.
But that's not the point, I was born in a house like anybody
else. After talking about the wogs and the niggers, You Gyppos,
he said, you are a funny lot. In the same breath, as you might say.
Don't you call me that, I said. What hurt me was him classing
me the same as all them others. Nobody calls me that, I said,
but I wasn't angry. I couldn't be, not with Mortimer. He just
sat there, looking at me straight, smiling a bit, and before I
knew it tears come into my eyes and Mortimer saw. You don't
want to take things so much to heart, was all he said. But he
never called me that again. Now I go on looking at him for a
bit, over the top of my cup. I only known him a month but it
seems like all my life.

'I been on this job a month now,' I say.

'So you have,' he says. 'You are a model of staying power,
Josiah.'

'I am fed up with it, matter a fact,' I tell him. 'It don't suit
my character.'

'You feel that it does not give you scope? Why not try a
change?'

'A change, that's it, I need a change.'

'You will never get the gold watch, Josiah.'

'What are you on about?' I ask him. Times like this I wonder
whether our friendship really means anything to Mortimer.
For all he knows I might be going to leave town.

All this time he has been letting his tea get cool—he never
drinks nothing hotter than tepid. He drinks half of it now in
one go, looking at me steady. 'That girl,' he says, 'the one who
came to the stall every night last week just when we were
closing, and you went off with her, what was her name, Joan
was it?'

'Not Joan, Joyce.'

'I knew it was something like that, I knew it was a name of that sort.'

'She's gone back to Wigan.'

'She didn't belong here then?'

'No, she come to spend a week with her married sister. I told you that before, Mortimer.'

'Did you? She's gone then, has she? Back to Wigan? You won't be getting it every night then. You're missing it, that's what it is. That's your trouble, mate, you are missing your shag.'

'Yes,' I say straight off without thinking. 'Yes, maybe that's it.' Truth is, I want Mortimer to think I was poking her, I don't want him thinking I never had no girls, not in the fullest meaning of the word, I mean. So I keep quiet a minute. Then I start thinking about Joyce. Nice grey eyes, she was a very shy girl, and her hands always warm and a bit dampish like in the palms, not wet, it's different to wetness. She cried on the last night, because the week was up. I've never done this for anyone before, she said. I've never opened my blouse for anyone before. She gave me her address written out on a piece of paper. Beautiful handwriting. There was education there, you could tell. Mortimer is smiling at me and I know he doesn't really believe I was poking Joyce every night. 'Well as a matter a fact I never got there,' I say, all in a rush.

'What?' he says. 'What do you mean?'

'If she'd of stayed another week maybe I'd of got there.'

It's a funny thing about Mortimer, you never know how he is going to take things. Now he is put out, I can tell by his face. He never wanted me to admit that about Joyce. Even though he never believed it in the first place. I can't understand this and it makes me feel sort of lost. He is the best friend I ever had, well I been travelling about since I was fifteen but I never met anyone like him, I mean he takes a real interest. So now I think the only way of getting back to where we was before is to tell him everything we done that last night.

'She wanted it,' I say. 'She wanted it all right, dying for it, but she was scared, see. She wouldn't lie down. We was down under the pier and I wanted her to lie down but she wouldn't. I was getting into her blouse like, but she said don't be rough, she said, and she undone all her blouse for me, undone it all herself. There you are, she said. She said I was the first bloke she ever undone her blouse for. All she had on underneath—'

'First man she undid her blouse for, I bet she's got a hole like the Mersey Tunnel,' Mortimer says in a kind of harsh way, not like his usual speaking voice at all, and now I am really lost. I don't know why he's getting so much against me, I don't know what I have done.

'I went out with her,' I say. 'You didn't.'

'Didn't need to,' he says, more quietly like. 'I could see it a mile off, there was no need for anything . . . tactual, Josiah, I never needed to fumble her up, no.'

'What do you mean?'

'You have to get things straight,' he says. 'You have to see things steady and see them whole. They will all try to tell you they are virgins. Any rotten old tart. Any old moribunda will tell you that, even in the midst of a standing shag from a syphilised seaman. With it in her up to the hilt, she'd still maintain.'

'What call have you . . .?' I say. He is moving now in spheres where I can't follow him. Anyway, Joyce never said nothing about being a virgin, she never used that word.

'Oh no,' he says. 'She couldn't ask you to deny your own eyes, could she?' He swallows the rest of his tea, then he starts smiling. 'Basing ourselves,' he says, 'on the proviso that the said jolly jack is actually shooting her a length at the moment of enquiry. No. She would say it was only the body, the *shell*, given over to base usages. Like all this when they say a certain woman is essentially innocent. She's had it through every orifice you could name and a few you couldn't but she is essentially innocent. *Untouched.* That is a lot of balls, Josiah, you take my word. I hate that kind of talk. I saw a couple having it once. Up against the side of a coffee stall. The woman was eating chips out of a packet. Youth at the prow and pleasure at the helm.'

As usual I don't know what to say. Mortimer has mastery of language like, he has a terrific flow of words in my opinion. But I still don't understand how you can tell anything just by looking. He never even talked to Joyce. I take a look at his face. He has a long face, long and narrow, with a long chin. His hair always very neat, short back and sides.

'Define your terms,' I say, playing for time like. (I heard a bloke say that once in a pub and I always remembered it.)

Mortimer's mouth always looks cold, I mean suffering from cold. His lips are very pale. You don't forget Mortimer's face.

'Define your terms,' I say.

'Take my word for it,' he says. 'That Joyce has seen more pricks than you've had hot dinners, Josiah. I bet they could bear witness in Wigan. We'd better be getting back. That old cow will be missing us.'

Simon ...

THE IDEA OF engaging a gardener was entirely my sister's. 'I have been to the Labour Exchange,' she said, spacing the words out, 'and I have notified them that a vacancy exists.' This while I was sociably, and in a cravat, having coffee with her on the terrace, on the first really warm day of the year; suffering, of course, as I always suffer, from the general abrasiveness of her attitudes and remarks, but concealing all offence as I wanted to discuss with her a boy that I had come upon shortly before in the grounds, roaming about at will, claiming to have permission. A boy with a bloody leg.

Before I saw him it was a day like any other. Whenever the weather is at all possible, and I include in that days of light drizzle and gusty days—indeed those jolly blowy days are just the thing—I spend the half hour between nine forty-five and ten fifteen in a certain corner of the grounds, carefully chosen to give me a view, on one side, of the drive for a short way, and on the other, of the little brick bungalow set quite on its own about three hundred yards off in the adjoining field. The bungalow belongs to a farm labourer whose wife, a woman not fat, but possessing generous proportions, is the reason for my stationing myself here so regularly. I wait to watch her sweep the concrete area at the front of the bungalow.

I am wearing my tunnelling suit of course; it is impregnated with clay, and the smell of dry clay rises to my nostrils, an intensely clandestine smell, seeming to contain the sum of all my secretive fevers in this little corner, screened by the hedge

on the field side and the road side and protected behind by an
abundant laburnum which was planted by my brother-in-law
Howard five years ago, shortly before he died. Altogether it is
what I call a jolly good hide.

I remain here, standing still, not thinking of anything in
particular. It is not silent, these grounds are never silent, not to
one who spends as much time in them as I do, but there are no
discordant noises. Let us say that it is May. I look up beyond
the laburnum, which of course is in flower. It is early enough
still for the clouds to have preserved their roseate, nacreous
look. High up in the sky I see gulls, the sun elicits flashes from
them as they turn. We are only five miles from the sea here.
Herring gulls, I name them, since they must be named, but
they are too far away to be identified with any certainty, invisible almost until the sunlight bursts on them and then they
seem not birds at all but particles of light.

All this time, while I look at the clouds, the gulls, the laburnum flowers, a feeling of apprehension grows in me as if I shall
be required to do something beyond my powers. The clay
smell of my person seems to intensify. Now, without exactly
looking across the field, I know that the woman has come
out. How shall I describe the effect on me of her appearance?
It is like shedding what is gross, looking deeply into a new
element. Six minutes past ten. She is wearing the red dress this
morning.

Now I need the binoculars. They are heavy ones, much too
heavy; twelve by forty, an excessive magnification; I was too
ambitious when I bought them. So heavy that it is impossible
for me, with my frail wrists, to hold them still. However I have,
in my cunning, cut a hole in the hedge two-thirds of the way
up, in which to rest them. I kneel to focus them, quickly, no
fumbling now. She is beginning. I am unwilling to miss the
smallest of her movements, not the least sketch or adumbra-
tion of a gesture would I forgo. Now I have her face
before me, distinct to the smallest detail, the dear brown
mole on the left cheek, the shiny skin below her eyes. All

around her still as ice, the house front, the bushes of the garden, all quite motionless, herself a figure of incessant activity with her little yellow brush. Now begins my familiar torment and ecstasy, the never being able to arrest her, to halt her in any one of the innumerable provocative postures of her body, and the inveterate hope that perhaps she might stop, remain still long enough to be properly seen, dwelt upon; or perhaps repeat one gesture frequently enough, one exact gesture frequently enough for the effect in the end to be static. It would be like a reiterated caress on some intimate part of my body. But it will never happen of course, each of her movements flows into the next for ever and ever.

This morning she begins sweeping from the left hand corner towards the centre, with her back to me. She bends, reaching with the brush to the farthest extent of her arm and the skirt of the red dress rises higher. I see the backs of her legs tauten as she reaches farther forward with the brush; irrepressibly the hope that she may remain thus rises in me, but already her arm has moved, sweeping towards her, and with this her body rises higher, the skirt is lowered some inches, she half turns, completing the movement of the sweeping, and now one leg is somewhat behind the other and bent at the knee so that I see the exact curve of the calf, the flesh of the inner thigh of her left leg, but before this can compose itself for me, it has dissolved into another, feet together, legs straightening, body almost upright then inclined again, facing me now, I see the crown of her head as she stoops, a pale irregular parting not quite in the middle and the loose dress falling away in front, so that I divine for one second the hang of her heavy breasts before her head is lowered farther, blocking my view, and before I can sharpen my excitement on the memory of what I think I have just seen—can it be true that she is not wearing a brassière?— her position has changed again, she has raised her head and I am looking at her thick white throat.

Now she stands upright. She has finished the sweeping and stands still for a moment or two looking out across the field behind the bungalow, which has been sown with wheat, a white-skinned, ample woman with untidy dark-brown hair and a round face and round brown eyes. I think she will be about thirty-five. I do not know her name. She has brought me often, and especially on windy days when I am vouchsafed incidental revelations, to the threshold of intense pleasure, and on occasion I have been enabled, kneeling in my little corner here, with the complicity of the laburnum—what would Howard think, I wonder?—to cross the threshold. I have never been nearer to her than I am now, I do not desire any closer proximity.

She goes back into the bungalow, leaving me with the accustomed feeling of desolation, the accustomed self-disgust. It is ten minutes past ten. I spend several more minutes here, in order to recover poise. Bees clot the laburnum flowers. The clouds are bleaching, no longer pearly, the seagulls have gone. From somewhere deeper in the grounds, towards the house, a yellow-hammer sings the first half of its refrain, then stops. A lazy singer. The binoculars I place in their case, which I strap bandolier-wise across my body. I emerge cautiously from my corner and begin to make my way across the grounds towards where my tunnel begins. I step very lightly crossing the drive in order that my feet make no sound on the gravel. The entrance to my tunnel is not more than a dozen yards from the edge of the drive, but I have chosen it with great care, it is screened from view completely by the enormous rhododendrons, indeed it is only by crawling under one of the bushes, right into the heart of it, that the entrance can be reached. . . .

Before leaving the drive I always glance about and pause. It is a measure of caution which has become a habit—on such habits my safety depends. Here on the drive I am part of the world of normality in which I arouse no, or only momentary, speculation, a resident of the house, standing on the gravelled drive of the house, a tall, thin, sharp-featured man, with thin sandy hair. In his late forties one would say. A conspicuous mildness of manner. No one can challenge me. But once having stepped over the tall plumy grasses that border the drive, once having stepped gingerly over, I am subject immediately to suspicion. What can he be doing? He is not gardening, a man who is gardening is unmistakable, he assumes an absolute right to be there, his behaviour is never secretive. I who am no gardener must always take care, I must never relax my vigilance. . . .

It was while I was still lingering there, enjoining on myself caution, that I heard it, the sound of clumsy human passage through vegetation. Someone not even attempting stealth. Someone *inside the grounds*. The realisation of this was so shocking that for some time after I was unable to move. The sounds had come from the direction of the road, not from the interior of the grounds. Between me and them were fifty yards or so of thick shrubbery, a group of birch trees and an ornamental pond. I paused a moment longer summoning resolution, then began to walk as quietly as possible diagonally through the shrubbery, aiming to emerge at the far right of the hedge that borders the road.

I saw him as soon as I emerged from the shrubbery into the open space that adjoins the hedge. A small boy with his blazered back to me, crouching slightly and looking up through the hedge, looking obviously for that local density against the sky that would denote a bird's nest. Intent on this he had not, it seemed, heard my approach, did not hear now my heavy breathing. He had on grey flannel shorts and his grey stockings had slipped down to his ankles. The whole side of his left leg, below the knee, was messy with blood.

I stood still, just inside the clearing, watching him, attempting to control my breathing, without much success. He seemed so unaware, it was difficult not to feel *myself* the interloper, *he* the one there by right. I said at last, not very loudly, 'What are you doing here?' The boy immediately straightened and turned. Cropped hair, a blunt puppy head, eyes small, deepset, blue. The side of his face had a shine as though smeared with something sticky, resin, sap, as though he had actually been thrusting his head into the vegetation, his whole head into it.

I felt predatory no longer, but invaded, this was alien life. 'What are you up to?' I said. 'Don't you know that this is private property?' The round face tightened briefly, almost with a grimace as though the face was too slack, without this preliminary, for speech, and then, instead of speaking, he looked away. 'I suppose you know,' I said, 'that you are trespassing actually?'

'I got permission,' the boy said. He had a husky voice.

'How can you have got permission?' I said. 'You are talking nonsense.' But a chill of doubt had already invaded me. Audrey, I thought immediately. *Audrey.*

'I am an observer,' the boy said.

'What on earth do you mean by that? You'd better clear off,' I said. What if I hadn't seen him, been away this particular morning—I have to leave the grounds sometimes. The creature had a sapper's, a burrower's head, and there was that shine on his face, he might easily have come upon my tunnel. The thought alone was sufficient to disturb my breathing once again. 'You'd better go,' I said, raising my hand and making a gesture as of waving on traffic.

The boy didn't move. 'I got permission,' he said again. 'From a lady in a red hat.'

'When was that?' A cunning question. I took some paces towards him.

'Day before yesterday, she said not to touch the trees but I could get bluebells.'

Good God, he had been wandering about, then, for days.

'I showed her my badge.'

'Badge,' I said. 'Badge?' In my agitation my eyes had begun watering. The boy turned the lapel of his blazer to show on the reverse side a small oval badge with some sort of emblem, ornate initials in blue. I peered forward but my vision was blurred. 'Badge?' I said again, peering vainly. I was in the grip of nightmare now, this creature had credentials.

The boy raised his head and said proudly, 'Royal Society for the Protection of Birds, Junior Branch. I am a member.'

He looked at me intently, still displaying the hideous insignia. 'I wrote away for it,' he said.

'I shall have to look into this matter.' I felt more confidence now that the badge had been explained. All the same, there was need for caution. Audrey must have given him permission to range about in the grounds. One of her moments of aristocratic largesse. Audrey was not in her right mind, of course. However it would be rash to countermand her instructions; if anything made her furious that did. . . . 'Well,' I said, nodding my head up and down, 'you can remain for the time being.' I began to withdraw, but found it impossible to turn my back on his victor's silence, so that I was still facing him, several yards away, when I stopped again. I simply could not leave him in possession, with his blunt burrower's head. 'No,' I said loudly. 'You must leave these grounds immediately. At once.' I again advanced upon him, making shooing motions with both arms. He regarded me for a moment, something changed in his expression—then he turned and began to make his way along the hedge towards the gate. 'And never come back,' I said, following at his heels. I followed him until I saw him through the gate on to the road. He had a bicycle there, propped against one of the concrete pillars of the gate. I watched him mount the bicycle and pedal slowly away in the direction away from the town. Except for him the road was quite empty in both directions, to the right, dead straight for over a mile, hazed on the horizon with thin summer mist, gradually disappearing into the flat and featureless arable plain, in the other direction, only visible for a hundred and fifty yards or so before turning sharply away to the left; beyond this bend was the bus-stop, the beginnings of the town.

I watched him diminish, disappear finally into the haze. For some time longer I stood there. Nothing passed on the road. Behind me in the choked grounds I sensed a multifarious life. It was mid-morning. From the folds of my person rose up a concentrated odour of clay. My tweed suit, originally green, is now a reddish colour owing to the impregnations of clay it has received in my passage to and fro along the tunnel. I thought for a moment, longingly, of the tunnel now, but I knew that I would have to see my sister first, get this matter of the boy cleared up. I began to walk again, still following the line of the hedge, until I reached the farthest corner of the grounds where the birch trees, planted close together, form a separate little copse with intermingling foliage. The earth here is moist, compounded with leaf mould, and it is soft underfoot. I come to a stop for no particular reason, look around, walk on again. I stop once more by the lily pond. This, like everything else, has been neglected of late years; it is reedy, fringed with green scum. The dark lily leaves float on the clear space where the scum has not encroached. There are huge Kingcups round the edges. From here, skirting the dense, the well-nigh impenetrable shrubbery in the centre of the grounds, I describe a wide curve through straggling rhododendron and azalea until I reach the fringe of rowan trees that separate the grounds from the rectangular lawn, the raised terrace beyond it and the house itself.

I stand in the shadow of the trees looking across the lawn at the house, which is of red brick with a long, low and pleasingly proportioned frontage, gabled at each end, the woodwork painted white, though the paint has blistered and flaked away in the years since Howard died, and some of the window frames have been warped out of shape. The grass of the lawn is knee high and smells still, despite the sun, of wet. My hands and my suit, and the earth around me are stippled with sunlight as the rays pierce through the thin leaves. The lawn beyond is dense, green, bright, without a stain of shadow. The wrought-iron chairs with their blue cushions wait on the terrace. Three Cabbage Whites, flying in a sort of formation, hover about the lawn nuzzling down into the tall grass for the shorter daisies. Not a grass moves but the whole area is clamorous with insects, from their throatless bodies contriving to emit a diversity of noises, whirrs, rasps, drum beats. The clay smell comes to my nostrils again, my essence, and I am assailed suddenly by a sensation familiar enough in childhood but of late years infrequent, a sort of displacement of personality. The boy pedals down the empty road, Audrey behind that brick façade brushes her hair, does something private to her appearance, oblivious of everything, Marion in the kitchen, wearing one of her light-coloured cotton dresses, prepares the coffee, in silence setting things out on a tray, the sky through the birch leaves is deep blue; where am I, from what point am I effecting these conjunctions?

I blink away these thoughts. I refocus. The house exposes its red brick front, its skeins of virginia creeper. Nothing moves in the house, nothing stirs the curtains, there is no sound of activity from within. Now, however, as though aware that a change of mood is necessary, Marion appears in a white dress, carrying the tray. I see the bright frizz of her hair in the sun-shine—she will inflict on herself these unbecoming home-perms—and sense, rather than see the care, the anxious parting of her lips as she sets the tray down on the wicker table. Poor Marion, her life bristles with obstacles. A moment later my sister comes through the french window on to the terrace, wearing a long-sleeved pale-blue dress. Her hair is a luminous silver-grey this morning, newly rinsed.

Audrey has coffee served to her at eleven o'clock every morning she is at home, taking it on the terrace when the weather is fine enough. But I am usually too busy in the grounds. Indeed, since the onset of spring, what with all the watching and the tunnelling I have not often made an appearance in the mornings. And to be perfectly truthful, if I had not had these reasons for absenting myself, I would have found others. I do not willingly consort with Audrey these days. There is some-thing very disturbing about her and I blame the Dramatic Society for it. Three years ago, that is about eighteen months after Howard's death, Audrey suddenly decided to join the Dramatic Society, although she has no acting ability whatever, and this connection with the theatre has had in my opinion harmful effects: her manner has grown steadily more artificial, she changes tone with startling abruptness, and furthermore she has lately become very extreme and precipitate in her actions. Take this matter of the hair, a small matter certainly, but symptomatic. I daresay there are women—perhaps it is a numerous class—who dye their hair grey, although I do not number any such among my acquaintance. If their hair is already greying they may do it, or if it is some hideous colour that needs to be changed. Audrey's hair in its natural state is a pleasant brown with no admixture of grey and she is not yet fifty; yet for the last year she has been dyeing it grey. And just three months ago, without a word to me or anyone, she went off to hospital to have her womb removed. There was nothing wrong with it at all; the doctor told me that. Considered solely as an organ it was perfectly healthy. Simply, Audrey no longer wanted to have a womb. That is what I mean by *precipitate*.

This morning, of course, I had to see her, because of the boy. I went round to the side of the house, skirting the lawn. About twenty yards of this route (the part adjoining the lawn itself) are clearly visible from the terrace, but my sister did not glance in my direction. I entered the house through the conservatory in the rear and went directly up to my room. I washed my hands and face and changed from my tunnelling suit (locking this up, as always, in a suitcase) into a blazer and flannels, donning also, as an afterthought, a maroon cravat. I think it was because of the cravat that as I plastered down at the mirror my somewhat dishevelled hair—my hair is very fine in texture and tends to wispiness, especially in the region above the ears—I began to feel quite debonair, a morning-coffee man. I was aware of course that this feeling was superficial, underlying it there was still the anxiety about the boy, but it persisted as I advanced towards Audrey across the terrace. True, I became a little flustered at the last moment, a familiar sense of unreality descended on me, but I attempted to disguise this—I think successfully—by making nonchalant motions with my hands.

'Ah Audrey,' I said. 'There you are. What a beautiful morning.'

She looked at my hands, which I had commenced to rub together, then at my face. Then, after a considerable pause— terribly disconcerting to me—she said, 'If it is coffee you want, Simon, you will have to go and get another cup from the kitchen.'

Involuntary as breathing, of course, this dryness of tone she immediately adopts in my expansive moments. She has been using it against me since she was seven and it is no less effective now than it was forty years ago.

'Something of the sort,' I said, attempting a genially indifferent tone. 'Something of the sort I had in mind.'

Rather moodily I went back into the house. Marion was sitting at the kitchen table, having a cup of coffee herself, and reading one of her *True Romance* magazines—it was on the table before her, open at a brightly coloured picture of a golden-haired girl sitting holding a letter under a flowering tree, musing. Marion is much addicted to these magazines, there are piles of them in her room as I noticed when, some months ago now, I obeyed an impulse of curiosity and went in there. Her elbows were resting on the table and her thin back was bent forward so that I could see, under the cotton dress, several of the little bumps of her spine. Her face when I entered was very close to the page and I thought that Marion probably should have her eyes tested; she has those warm, brown, very gentle eyes that often seem to weaken early. She straightened in her chair as I approached her and looked round and smiled in her vague startled way, then looked away again immediately. She never seems to look at anything or anyone for more than a second or two as though further scrutiny would reveal too much, bring something irrevocably into the open. I smiled at her. 'It's all right,' I said. 'I only want a cup and saucer. I can get them myself.' Marion brings out some vestigial protective instinct in me. If Howard had lived she would not have been left to her own devices so much, she would not have devoted her leisure to home-perms and *True Romances*. Howard took her in at twelve when her mother died (her father had deserted them some years before this). The mother was related to him, though not very closely, and he had plans for her education, but then he died and Audrey got involved with the Dramatic Society and nothing was done for Marion at all except that Audrey taught her how to sew and bake cakes, things like that; now, of course, Audrey looks down on the girl because she is uncultivated, she uses her as a sort of servant really, and lately she has taken to shouting at her and even slapping her on occasion. So although I never say much to Marion we have a kind of alliance because we are both subject to Audrey's tyranny.

I got the cup and saucer and carried them carefully back to the table on the terrace. Audrey was looking out over the grounds. She did not turn her head. Pouring, I regarded the backs of my hands. I have fingers that are best described as spatulate, with neat nails, despite all my digging, and im-maculate half-moons. The veins on the backs of my hands were unhealthily distended this morning.

I sipped my coffee, resisting thoughts of my imminent dissolution, watching Audrey who had continued to look out over the lawn. Her face had that semblance of a slight smile it always wears in repose, an accidental upward tendency of the corners of the mouth. I have never known a face less diffident, less expressive of doubt than Audrey's, less vulnerable to surprise attack. The set of the mouth, the unvarying order of her hair, the level, very narrow grey eyes all combine to give her the appearance of someone who has discounted in advance whatever one has to impart, however startling. If this is what is meant by poise, she has it.

It doesn't deceive me, of course. There are these plunges of hers, that I have mentioned already. And latterly she has screamed quite often in her sleep.

'Do you know what I saw this morning in the grounds?' I began, in what I thought was an arresting tone, but she continued for some moments more to look calmly out at the overgrown lawn, and I saw from the slowness of her movements as she raised the cup and something consciously queenly about the set of her head, that she had fallen into her Prospero part, confronting with unimpaired dignity the uncouth communications of this Caliban. Since she became a member of the Dramatic Society Audrey's grip on reality has weakened. And not only that: she brings dreadful people to the house now. That very evening, I suddenly recalled, the whole committee of the Dramatic Society was coming to supper.

'What did you see then, Simon?' my sister said at last, with an indulgent, governessy inflection.

'I saw a squirrel,' I said. 'In the grounds. One of those little red fellows.' I had not meant to say this. It broke from me at the last moment, because of nervousness and an ingrained dislike of direct communication. And I was conscious of its inadequacy after my preliminary tone. I attempted to fill the gap with further gestures of the hand, but could feel her eyes upon me.

'Is that all?' she said.

'I saw a boy,' I said, 'there was a boy in the grounds this morning. I sent him packing, of course. You know he actually—' I infused my tone with laughter, suddenly seeing how totally mistaken I had been to bring up the subject at all.

'Did your boy have a badge?' she asked. 'A badge he was eager to display?'

'He had some such thing, some wretched thing on the reverse side of his lapel. As though that entitled him—'

'It must be the same boy I met some days ago as I was going down the drive. I told him he could get bluebells.'

'Yes, but you didn't give him permission, did you, to wander about the grounds at will?' Despite myself a certain asperity had crept into my tone, and Audrey noticed it, as I could tell by an extra sort of stateliness that now began to settle over her.

'I may well have done,' she said, beginning to space her words out more, to show her command of the situation.

'But my dear Audrey,' I said, aiming at a tone of easy expostulation. I had, however, begun to tremble slightly.

She raised one arm, rather languidly, I watched it go up in apparent slow motion, an arm clad to the wrist in pale-blue jersey—the paler shades of blue she affects greatly—culminating in a plump creased wrist, plump white fingers. Despite a certain avidness of temperament, my sister's hands do not resemble talons, but have instead a too human look, a rather horrifying plumpness. They are hands you could almost call chubby. She had indicated the swarming lawn, the thickets and tangles of the grounds beyond. 'All this land,' she said, 'for the use of only two people, two people getting old, Simon? The land is for all, land is like love, it is not divisible, you can build fences, of course, but basically I mean, land is not divisible.'

I strove to maintain an appearance of dispassion. 'Why not then throw the place open to picnickers, trippers, have a coach park built and, save the mark, urinals? Why stop at one smelly boy?' Such rhetoric always annoys me, such superior self-enhancing views, requiring no sacrifice. I blame the Dramatic Society for Audrey's constant adopting of these attitudes nowadays. Territory and property, things inalienably one's own, are necessary, all these sharers have been half-baked from the Galilee lot onwards. She should see my robins, they could show her whether land is divisible or not, haven't I seen them fight for land till they were blind with blood? Of course for Audrey there is no threat, no challenge, no need to fly at anybody's eyes. The house and grounds are hers for her lifetime. Anyone who, like myself, occupies his territory only provisionally and on sufferance will understand my feelings as I looked at her closed complacent face. 'You are being sentimental,' I said. A wounding word, which I saw at once, and with immediate alarm, had gone home. Some of Audrey's stateliness deserted her. She looked at me more narrowly. And when she spoke her voice was much less leisurely.

'There is another thing I have to tell you,' she said. Another thing? What had the first been? Suddenly I knew that a disastrous new *fiat* was about to be uttered. With an instinct of postponing the moment I set down my cup and rose to my feet. I said some words in an incoherent manner and adjusted the set of my cravat.

'I can't hear you,' Audrey said. 'No, just a minute Simon, if you don't mind. There is something you ought to know. I have been to the Labour Exchange.'

'The Labour Exchange?'

'Howard kept the place up while he lived. The grounds and so on. It was a model of its sort in those days, for many years a model, everyone agreed. There were arbours and bowers in the grounds then, seats disposed about. What has happened since to them I don't know. They *were* there.'

'And are still,' I said.

'Somewhere, no doubt, in the . . . herbage, they are still. All those improvements Howard introduced, all that work gone for nothing.'

'I keep things in check,' I said, 'in a number of small, perhaps imperceptible ways. . . .'

'All gone for nothing. Sometimes I could break down altogether Simon, and weep, yes weep. You, of course, do nothing. The grounds could revert to immemorial forest, primeval swamp. You would merely watch, through your binoculars, the alligators or parakeets. Perched in some ridiculous hide. You won't play a man's part, Simon. So I have been to inform them that a vacancy exists.'

'A vacancy,' I repeated, still not understanding. I had for some reason a vision, at this word, of a breach, something like a broken window or a gap in the hedge, something that might need repairing.

'They assured me that they would send a reliable man.'

Now at last I understood. She had been behind my back to the Labour Exchange to ask for someone. 'You have been to ask for a gardener,' I said, in a voice that was not completely under my control.

'Not a gardener, exactly, Simon,' she said, and now she had reverted to that domineering leisureliness. 'A handy-man.'

I could find absolutely nothing further to say. I began to retreat across the terrace, making, in order not to seem too shaken, some farewell gestures. Audrey went on talking just as if I had not moved: 'It is not as though we need a *skilled* gardener, not at this stage. There is dead wood to be cleared, weeds of every sort to be uprooted. A person sufficiently robust is what we need. Of course I did not explain all this to the officials at the Labour Exchange. . . .'

I descended from the terrace and went quickly round the corner of the house. I went straight upstairs and changed out of my morning-coffee kit into my tunnelling suit. It is quite possible for one who knows, by taking a circular route on the west side of the house, to reach the heart of the grounds without at any time coming into view from the terrace. This I did. I was making, of course, for my tunnel; that was the only place where such a shock could be even partially absorbed.

My tunnel extends from the point in the midst of the rhododendrons that I have already mentioned, diagonally across the grounds for about seventy-five yards, avoiding the denser areas of vegetation, but always adequately screened. From one point or other along it I can command a view of the whole central area of the grounds and also the house front including the terrace and lawn. I am hoping this summer, or *was* hoping before this bombshell of Audrey's, to continue it another twenty or thirty yards right up to the hedge that runs along the road. If I could succeed in this, I should be able to watch from the bottom of the hedge, the girls cycling past at weekends, careless of their skirts on the empty road, their legs moving up and down, up and down. I adore the abandoned leg movements of cycling girls.

It is not really a tunnel, of course, but rather a roofed trench. It has taken me two years to complete this much of it. I am no longer sure what led me to excavation. Delight in the work for its own sake has to a large extent obscured my original motives.

However, it is certainly true that some months after Howard's death Audrey began to tamper with my belongings. She was entering my bedroom in my absence, handling my books. My room was kept locked, of course, but anyone can have a key duplicated. When I returned there was always some slight change in the appearance of things, a modified aspect; nothing definitely displaced, she was too cunning for that. I devised small traps for her, like placing one of my hairs across Bentley's *Birds of the British Isles* in such a way that anyone opening the book must infallibly have disarranged it: when I returned the hair was exactly in place. Nevertheless I could not be deceived, there was always something subtly different in the appearance of things when I returned to my room. Such care to cover her traces was particularly menacing. It became plain to me that, Howard gone, Audrey was attempting to take over my life.

So I hit on the idea of excavating a subterranean room in the grounds and moving the objects I most valued into it. The trench was necessary because a concealed approach to the room was necessary. Like most truly artistic conceptions it grew magnified in the execution: I extended the trench further and further as the unique opportunities for observation that it conferred became clear to me. . . .

In the more shaded parts of the grounds dew has not dried on the dock leaves and flowering nettles. Spiders' webs glitter in every thread. I move forward cautiously, and now I am among the rhododendrons, screened, invisible. Quickly now I go down on hands and knees, crawl into the heart of the rhododendron bush, the bitter smell of the leaves fills my nostrils. The entrance here is simply a square of tarpaulin lightly covered with earth. It can be removed in one piece. I remove it, and insert my body down into the hole, replacing the cover immediately, and with great care so as not to dislodge the earth. Now I am in complete darkness. I take from my jacket pocket the small electric torch which never leaves my person, proceed at a shuffle along the trench. The trench is narrow so my arms are constricted, and the roof is a good twelve inches lower than my full height which obliges me to crouch and incline my head. The thin beam of the torch lights up the walls of the tunnel, in some places smooth, in others pitted with small holes. The smell of clay is very strong. I proceed at a steady shuffle, head down, watching in the torchlight the motions of my brown brogues. Here and there I notice with some disquiet the gleam of wet: water is getting in from somewhere. Flooding is what I dread most. Repairs are constantly necessary, the canes I have used for the roof become brittle and have to be replaced, the sods waste and show a suspiciously geometrical line of rot. However, for considerable stretches there has been a completely successful integration of foreign and local matter, a solid roof has been formed that could be trodden on without damage.

I continue until I reach the side turning and now I have to go on hands and knees for a few yards, this tunnel is very low, descending steeply to a circular pit, about six feet in diameter. It is this I call my underground room. I have had to buttress the roof of this tunnel and that of the pit itself with poles to prevent caving in. It is only four feet from the floor to the ceiling so I generally find it more convenient, while down here, to go on hands and knees. I crawl over to the corner and light the oil lamp that rests in the recess in the wall. Now I have need no longer for a torch. The rosy light from the lamp illuminates my bookshelf, cut into the clay and lined with felt and oilcloth, with its row of bird-books and my collection of advertisements for ladies' silk stockings, the Monet nude over the wall, whose yellow skin and complete unconcern I find deeply satisfying, the wooden stool and the strip of red linoleum on the centre of the floor. All these things I have gradually, and with immense labour, conveyed here.

I sit on the stool and look straight before me. Only here do I experience real peace. The roof is at least four feet thick and the ground above in any case inaccessible as I have taken care to excavate below the thickest part of the shrubbery. Not many can have a room such as this, as private as an undivulged idea or desire. Except for my heart there is no sound at all. I inhale the clay smell. I wonder if a wireless might be feasible. Strains of music might be faintly audible to anyone in the vicinity above. They would doubt their senses. Like the god leaving Anthony. ... Gradually, as I sit here, all strain and anxiety leave me. The problem of the gardener I deliberately postpone.

I was still postponing it at half past six that evening, when I took up my usual position in the corner of the grounds. At half past six or thereabouts the woman in the bungalow across the field is quite often preparing herself to go out. And while she is in the midst of this preparation it may be that her husband calls out for something or she remembers something she has left elsewhere, hair-pins, stockings, something of that sort. These interruptions in her toilet cause her to pass quite frequently from bedroom to living-room, and on these warm evenings, with the front door open, there are prospects of incidental revelations. She feels secure, of course, so far from the road. And this element of confidence, of unconcern, is an important, indeed an essential one. I used at one time to go up to London as frequently as I could afford it to see what are called *tableaux*, the enactment by nude persons of mythological scenes, but I used to feel resentful, sitting in the dark, *sharing*, and then there was the complicity of the performers themselves, I disliked that intensely. No, there has to be unawareness. One evening last June, she stood for quite three minutes dressed only in bra and pants right in the open doorway. That incident, and the brief sojourn of a pair of hoopoes among the apple trees behind the house, were the highlights of last year.

This evening I positioned myself there more from habit than anything else. I was still shaken by the edict of my sister's, the effort of keeping the binoculars steady was greater than usual, and in the event I saw nothing but the flash of bare arms briefly raised in the bedroom. However, had I not been there, standing there beside the hedge, at a few minutes to seven, I should not have witnessed the passing through the gates of Mrs King and I should probably have forgotten once again that this evening was the supper party for the members of the Dramatic Society committee. Mrs King has a square, mannish face, flushed at this moment from the exertion of walking; she is wearing a belted blue raincoat of a sort that defies lecherous speculation even more efficiently than it excludes the wet. Mrs King has almost no neck. In the plays put on by the Drama Group she is experienced, maternal, *décolletée*, with powdered shoulders, wearing strings of what will pass for pearls. It is surprising how, whatever the play, the members of the Dramatic Society seem always to enact the same roles and dress in the same manner. I make a point of seeing these productions because I am convinced that Audrey's aberrations need to be carefully watched. I slip in when the play has started and leave before the end. If my presence there has been noted Audrey has never mentioned it. She has not been given, up to now, any but the most minor roles.

Mrs King is followed after some moments by Miss Gravelin and Mr Dovecot who have presumably met by chance in the vicinity. They are both reacting in their different ways to the accident of being together; Dovecot angular and jugular with a thin and melancholy nose. Gravelin pony-tailed, aiming at the junoesque, stepping on her large feet as though about to launch on a ballet sequence, with a nose and chin that are always too neighbourly, too eager to meet. These two are accustomed to provide whatever romantic interest the play contains: she with an unvarying brand of archness, he too frantic in the region of the Adam's apple. They pass along the drive, Gravelin talking continuously about some people she has apparently been staying with in Edinburgh, looking straight ahead; Dovecot inclined towards her, his long straight hair flopping down over his brow. She is wearing, I notice chiefly, a skirt with a pattern of what seem to be pineapples, though mauve in colour, he a clerkly sort of suit. They pass out of sight but Gravelin's voice I hear some moments longer; 'And they always called me

Annie, never Anne. My name of course is Anne, but they always said *Annie,* as you might say Jeanie or Joanie. . . . ' Gravelin's conversation centres almost always round some one of her own attributes.

Major Donaldson and Miriam Daintry still to come. I wait there for five or six minutes more, but nothing happens. The bungalow door is shut, its windows dark and inexpressive. The sun has set and in the luminous pallor of the sky beyond the bungalow, numbers of swifts are wheeling. I set off walking up the drive towards the house. Just before the final bend I hear the sound of a car approaching. I stand well to the side and wait. It is Donaldson in his green Rover. I catch a glimpse of a tweed cap, a silvery moustache. He toots his horn to me. I begin a sort of wave then at the last moment convert this into a military salute, coming at the same time to attention.

Only Miriam now. She will arrive late, of course, make an entrance. Her eyes heavily made up in an oriental fashion, her temple-bell earrings. She aims at the exotic but misses at the extremities, having large coarse hands and no ankles to speak of. She is my sister's *friend.* She plays fallen women or apparently wicked women with pasts full of sin and shame and wardrobes full of black velvet dresses, who in the end sacrifice themselves for love. I am visited now, as I approach the house, by a rush of detestation for Miriam: it is she I am sure I have to thank for this decision of Audrey's to engage a gardener. I can hear them discussing it, over coffee, at the Metropole at a corner table with a view of the sea. Entering the house, mounting the stairs I become convinced that this is so, I see Miriam in a cossack hat and knee-length boots—it is March let us say—speaking with the inane vehemence of her sort in the restaurant of the Metropole: 'My dear you must have it seen to, people are beginning to *notice,* it is so overgrown.' Nodding her Cossack head. 'You owe it to dear Howard's memory, have you thought of it in that light?' And my sister, my sister would say, 'Do you really think so?', enjoying her role of lonely little woman, her will coiled up tight as a steel spring inside her. . . .

I unlock my bedroom door and enter. I wash and change into my grey pinstripe suit. I shall have to attend this supper party, of course, however unattractive the prospect and however unwelcome my presence. After this bombshell of Audrey's I cannot afford to neglect anything.

In the hall, however, I hesitate. Voices come to me from the drawing-room, Miriam Daintry's among them; she has arrived then. I experience a sudden painful emotion, almost like grief, at my isolation. Their tones as they talk together are no more divisible, no more individually meaningful to me than the clamour of rooks or frogs. I am not of the tribe.

I overcome this feeling and pausing only to check the elegant inch of shirt below my cuff, I enter the room. Conversation ceases immediately, there is a hush. Nobody of course has been expecting me to appear, least of all Audrey. It has become tacitly agreed between us that on such occasions, when she is *entertaining*, I shall keep away. Now I have created an awkward situation. I make gestures of salutation to the seated committee members, and once more check my cuffs.

'So glad you were able to join us, Simon.' Audrey takes her duties as hostess very seriously. I can see the lines of strain conflicting with her gracious smile. She is flushed along the cheek bones. 'Get yourself a drink,' she says. 'You know where everything is.' I am surprised at understanding these words easily when outside the door I had felt so excluded; I do not believe her words are aimed at me, however: it is a fragment detached from the tribal colloquy, a fragment unexpectedly intelligible.

'Evening, Thebus,' the Major says. 'How are you keeping?'

'Fair to middling,' I say in a bluff forthright manner. 'How's yourself, Major?' Turns of phrase which, five minutes before, I could not have conceived myself employing. I move over to the sideboard against the wall. The drinks are at the near end of it, food covers the rest. Marion has been busy all day with this. I cast my eye over it: ham, beef, brawn on great oval dishes flanked by mustard and chutney: the usual concomitants of salads, gleaming and oleaginous; a wooden board with various cheeses, riddled, fissured or smooth; a wicker bowl of fruit. Pride of place, right in the centre, goes to the vast dome-shaped chocolate mousse, darkly shining on its platter. Measuring out my gin, I eye the glistening slopes of the mousse; motionless now but infinitely impressionable, on the brink or at the last throb of some diapason of wobbles and quakes. Behind me I hear the conversation picking up again with:

Yes, the voice was impressive, considered as a voice—
Marvellous voice we thought, but as it turned out—
We thought give him a try for heaven's sake—
Absolutely calamitous, yes—
He couldn't walk on even—
He didn't know what to do with his hands—
He couldn't look anybody in the eye—

The words of the tribe. As self-contained as the dome of mousse. He sounds remarkably like myself, the man they are discussing, except for the marvellous voice. My own voice is remote and reedy. One of the most ancient of shapes, the dome. The shape of the heavens as it seems to mortals. The shape of the Dramatic Society. How dare they exclude me in this way. How dare Audrey allow boys to roam at will, engage gardeners behind my back. My tunnel, two years' work, threatened because of this whim. Resentment rises in me, and the desire for revenge. Why should I always be on the outside of everything, appreciating my exclusion with an aesthetic ache? Suddenly I see a way, tempting but alarming too, I see a way of compelling this world to contain me. My back is on their tribal twittering, I am holding my gin and tonic, looking fixedly at this Womb of Being, this chocolate mousse. Its perfection of shape increases my antagonism. Quickly I glance over my shoulder. No one is looking at me. I can struggle against temptation no longer. It is the work of a moment to raise my hand to my mouth, as if to suppress a belch or yawn, extract the false teeth from my upper jaw and drop them delicately and quite irrevocably into the very centre of the mousse, which now at this test demonstrates its superb lightness of texture—we certainly have a treasure in Marion—by parting with what I swear is the faintest of hisses and sighs, admitting the teeth and closing over them almost completely—the slightest of indentations. It is really as though my teeth are made welcome.

Mistaking my immediate panic for exhilaration I turn about briskly, intending to insert myself into the conversation too, with some remarks about bird song in our local woods, but realise immediately that I cannot now speak to anyone nor indeed invite close scrutiny. There are a number of consonants I cannot now pronounce without a rather disgusting sibilance. Decidely I am *hors de combat*.

This sense of physical disability intensifies my alarm. I begin to wish very much that I had not dropped my teeth into the mousse. Still holding, or to be more exact clutching my glass, I leave the sideboard and saunter over to a corner of the room out of the direct light. Here I sit, a little turned away, presenting the right side of my face. The conversation is continuing:

'It brings me back to a point I've made before, if you ladies will bear with me. . . .' That is the Major, isn't it, yes, leaning forward in his grey flannel suit, hitching up the trousers slightly, getting ready to give the ladies a briefing. I wonder again what he can be doing in this *galère*. He plays butlers and business men and fathers of rebellious children, with uniform woodenness. What does he want with all this after the years of pink gins and mild curries, talk of promising popsies and conscientious corporals, indoor rugby on Regimental Dinner Nights, snoozing in leather armchairs in Cairo, Camberly, Gib, his hold on the air-mail edition relaxing?

'What we need is a professional producer, someone with the professional know-how—'

'Oh, but Major Donaldson.' Audrey leans forward too,

moving her shoulders under the lilac-coloured cardigan. 'Oh, but our amateur status is the thing about us really, isn't it? I mean, this is our *thing*, not being commercial in any way. . . .' A professional might be coarsely commercial enough to tell her she can't act.

'Quite right, my dear.' Snap of thin lips, Miriam Daintry. She wants no outsiders either, no lessening of power. She put thoughts of a gardener into Audrey's head, I am convinced of it. *I hope she gets the teeth.* I hope no one gets the teeth. It was madness to drop them into the mousse. Bound to be detected. Unless—and here I see a modicum of hope—unless they have sunk too deep to be reached in the course of first helpings. Surely after all that ham and beef and potato salad no one will be clamouring for seconds of mousse? I notice in myself increasing symptoms of unease. My palms moisten, I have a tendency to yawn.

'I remember once working for a professional producer. It was in Nottingham.' Ah yes, that is Gravelin, attempting to reclaim the conversation from these abstractions. 'Very competent, of course, but outside of work he was a terror.' Her large shining eyes play over us. We are meant to be wondering about the relations between Gravelin and this terrible producer outside of work. After the statutory pause she will enlighten us, at length. *I hope Gravelin gets the teeth.*

'He was like all these very artistic people, he couldn't resist beauty, simply couldn't keep—'

She is cut off by Audrey who says with the gracious smile I know so well, 'Professionalism, I think, is the curse of much of our life today, don't you think so, Major?'

'What do you think, Thebus?' asks the Major, taking me completely by surprise. 'You're a man of the world.'

This unexpected question, coming at a time of grave misgiving and physical disability, is almost too much for me. I am almost overcome. I control myself, however, stiffen my twitching features and, keeping my head averted and my upper lip as motionless as possible, pronounce the word 'Definitely'

—all sounds within my present range. There is a longish pause, as though people are expecting something further, but I sit with my face averted, gazing fixedly at a painting of moorland ponies on the wall. I attempt a gesture of finality, forgetting the gin, some of which spills on to my trousers. After several more moments stark scrutiny of ponies and heather, I hear Audrey saying, 'Shall we have supper now?' Intent on saving the situation. People gather round the sideboard, return to their places with heaped plates. There they sit, knees together under napkins. I can eat nothing, of course, but must make some pretence. There is beer and there is burgundy, but I have no heart for either. My gaze returns repeatedly to the ponies.

Gravelin waits till people are helpless, their mouths full of salad, and then begins again. Now she is speaking about the tender and beautiful relationship she has with her mother.

'No thank you, dear lady,' I hear the Major say. 'No more. It was very good indeed, excellent. Mousse? Well, yes, perhaps a little. . . .'

Now for it. Of course, had I said at the time with light laughter, Oh, how silly of me, my teeth have fallen into the mousse, I shall have to dig them out, so sorry, what a *contretemps*, then it might have passed off. Simply, no one could then have partaken of the mousse; the symmetry of the feast would have been destroyed. But an asymmetrical feast is not so bad as a traumatic one. Now it is too late.

I watch the Major furtively as he freights his spoon with mousse, conveys it up towards the silver-grey moustache. No foreign body there. Others now are accepting mousse, everyone it seems is eager to get at it. Except Gravelin, whom talking has delayed.

'I am hungry,' she says, 'around about supper time, generally speaking, around about this time, yes, I *will* have a little more ham, quite delicious, thank you.'

I rise, carry my untouched plate to the sideboard where I leave it in an inconspicuous place. Making use of the large spoon left there for the purpose, I help myself to an enormous heap of mousse. I probe into the heart of what remains, but feel no obstruction. The teeth are already served then, already dished out. Perhaps, perhaps in mine. I return to my place in the corner, attack the mousse immediately, nothing, nothing at all. The glutinous stuff, darkly glistening, mocks my spoon with its lack of resistance, sweetly dissolves against my toothless gums. I see Mrs King finishing off her mousse with dainty licks, nothing there either. Feelings of excitement and apprehension sweep through me in equal measure. It is like seeing humanity for these few moments *sub specie aeternitatis*. We are all doomed, of course, but one of us is more immediately singled out. People are finishing now, perhaps the teeth have not been served out after all, perhaps—no, Gravelin has not finished yet, in fact has hardly started. A mound of mousse still on her plate. Without ceasing to present a rigid profile to the room, I am able to watch Gravelin out of the corner of my eye. I would like to leave the room but a sort of fascination prevents me.

'My mother,' Gravelin says, laying down her spoon for a moment, 'makes me these huge breakfasts which I cannot eat. I am never hungry in the mornings. I do not like to refuse, as it hurts her feelings.'

'A good way of raising funds,' I hear Audrey say, very earnestly, 'would be to organise a raffle. We could use the grounds of this house for it. Invite a lot of people for tea in the grounds, well a sort of garden party, you see, charge them quite a lot for tickets, and give a prize for the winning number. You could use these grounds, willingly. It would have the additional advantage—'

'She would never understand, you know,' Gravelin says. 'She would never—' She begins to pay a more particular attention to her plate. She makes small stabbing motions with her spoon. Her face expresses a sort of absorption.

'You could get a small polythene bag,' says Dovecot, speaking for the first time. He is interested, it seems, in Gravelin's breakfast predicament. 'Scoop it in when your good mother isn't looking, plenty of bins on the way to work, or you could keep it for your elevenses.'

She makes no reply. As yet of course it is merely an unidentified solid, acceptable as a bone if this were soup, inexplicable however in mousse. She prods at it further, separates it further from the mass.

'I must say that this a most generous offer,' Donaldson says to my sister.

'Well, I often think, you know, all this land for only two people, two people getting old, it doesn't seem—'

With dismay I see incredulity turn into a sort of anguish on Gravelin's large face. I have the impression of watching her gorge rise as you might watch mercury in a thermometer. She stands up, holding her plate. Her napkin falls.

'It would go into your handbag,' Dovecot says. 'One of those small polythene bags.'

'There is a denture in my pudding,' Gravelin says, almost casually, uttering, immediately after, a single sweet-toned gulp or sob and clapping her free hand over her mouth.

'What *can* you mean?' Audrey says, standing up in her turn.

'Ugh!' says Gravelin, starting off on a series of shudders, and of course I do not underestimate the nastiness of that sight, the yellowish teeth and pale pink palate all beset with mousse.

Now Gravelin is surrounded. They are all looking at her plate. 'Dashed funny thing, that,' I hear Donaldson say. I remain seated with my stiff upper lip, but when Gravelin starts laughing, I watch the plate taken from her wavering hand, put hurriedly down on a small table not far from me.

'Ha, ha, ha,' laughs Gravelin, on an ascending scale, shaking in the grip of Miriam and my sister, her pony-tail flopping grotesquely. She draws in her breath very noisily, giving glimpses of frantic activity in the region of the glottis. Her eyes look straight before her.

I am frightened and delighted at this hysteria of Gravelin's.

Never before have I witnessed such commotion in a human throat. There is no time, however, to be lost. Move along the wall to the table, take up with trembling hand the slippery teeth. Into the trouser pocket with them. Gravelin still the centre of attention. Nobody sees me leave.

Josh ...

WHAT FINALLY DONE it was this dumb bloke, coming up and making a scene on the stall. I was still in two minds, I hadn't decided nothing, but I felt better like, since Mortimer said that about needing a change. He agreed with me, I mean. I had to wait till pay day anyway. There wasn't no hurry. Then this dumb bloke come up, well for all I know he was deaf and all. He could make noises. Thursday night it was, just beginning to get dark. I'm not convinced in my own mind they should let these sort of people out, that's what Mortimer says anyway. He wanted a go on the rifles, well you can't bar them, can you, they've got the money. He got hold of the gun like he'd never seen one before. Pointing it all over the place, he was. That's *dangerous*. One of them pellets through your eye, that's all you need. Steady on mate, I told him. Friendly like. Don't point your gun up there, I told him. You got no quarrel with the heavens. Course I don't know if he understood me. He was moving his mouth all the time, stretching it like, and these big brown eyes of his looking straight at me, never mind where the gun was pointing. Mortimer laughed when I said that about the heavens. There's your target, Jack, I said to him. He had his shots, a bob's worth, nothing happened, but he swore down on the last shot that he'd hit the bull. What I mean by swore down, this stretching got all speeded up and he started making these loud noises and bringing his face up near to mine. Listen, I said, but I don't know if he could even *hear*, listen, when you hit the bull the light goes on and your picture is took.

In your case mate this did not happen. But he wouldn't have it. He started thumping himself on the chest and pointing at the target, making these noises all the time, gaar—gaar—gaar, thick and bubbly like it was coming through water. Like he was gargling. He kept getting his face up close and *pleading*, no other word for it, and his eyes, he had these big brown eyes, dozy eyes they'd be usually but now they looked as if he had a pain. Why he wanted a picture of himself holding a rifle, I do not know. Maybe he had a girl friend, they've got their instincts a course, like anybody else.

Anyway people come crowding round, what a crying shame, cheating a poor defenceless dumb bloke. It was bad for business so Mrs Morris said give him his money back but don't let him have another go. That's what I done but I tell you I won't forget him in a hurry, them eyes of his and them noises. I decided there and then, this is not the job for me. I mean it was *disgusting*.

What I thought afterwards was, it wasn't just whether he hit the bull or not, a bloke would not plead with you over a thing like that, no, it was the whole situation, he was asking me to put things right for him. His *faculties*. Maybe he could of had plastic surgery if it could of been caught quick enough, I dunno. I couldn't get this feeling over to Mortimer, he wouldn't see it, besides I can't express myself too well, that's my trouble. Mortimer knows a lot and the thing about it is, he has a wide vocabulary. I personally think Mortimer will make a contribution one of these days. He said blokes like that, cripples and blokes without their *faculties*, should be kept away from healthy people. They are an affront, he said. His own words. But, I said, Mortimer I said, this bloke was looking at me as if I could give him his faculties back again, what I mean is—It is no use trying to feel what a dumb bloke feels, Mortimer said, and his eyes got bigger because I was arguing like, he hates to be argued with. Well I got scared when I seen that, I hate Mortimer to be angry with me, he might just decide to stop being my friend and once he did that I know he'd never change, it would be for good. You are taking the sentimentalist line, he said. Haven't you ever heard of neecher? Neecher? I said. Define your terms. Slave morality, he said, looking at me with those big eyes.

Well I saw a way to get back on the right side of him and that was by saying things against this dumb bloke. Don't ask me how I knew this but it turned out right. His eyes was nearly coming out of his head, I said, and them noises he made, well, I said, what it reminded me of was a bloke trying to shit and couldn't. He liked this, I could tell. Just like a bloke straining to shit and couldn't, I said. That was what he was like, and eyes like piss holes in the snow.

Mortimer liked this. He laughed and he went back to a more normal look. That's right, he said. What songs the sirens sang and what a deaf and dumb bloke feels are equally beyond the bloody pale. Well, I couldn't follow him here but I didn't let on, a course. You got to keep a sense of humour, in our job, I said. Haven't you, Mortimer? All the same, I said, I think I'd like a change. I'm going to the Labour, day after tomorrow, see what they got on their books.

I couldn't tell from his face what he thought about this, whether he was put out or not. He didn't say nothing. You said I needed a change, I said. You did say that, didn't you Mortimer?

Simon ...

WITHIN THE SMALL enclosure formed by the shrubs it is hot. Light slides over the leaves, glosses the magnolia flowers ahead of me a little to the right. Beyond this I can see yellow sickles of forsythia. Trees that go on flowering in spite of all neglect. My arm and shoulders are flecked with sunlight filtering down through the leaves, no doubt my head also and all my prone body. My eyes will be about eight inches from ground level.

I raise the binoculars and the world blurs, melts, develops a sort of weeping or running grain. Looking thus through the unfocused lenses, I could easily forget my humanity, my element. My hands begin to tremble with the weight. I place the leather case on the ground before me and rest the binoculars on it, tilted slightly upwards. I spend some time focusing, then, beautifully clear and distinct, quite still, a section of hedge, hawthorn and hazel, the fresh green of brambles. . . .

Almost immediately I see the robin, not at the nest but a little beyond it on the lowest branch of a hazel. The robin is deforming itself for love. Breast feathers puffed out, it edges along the branch, tail stiff and vertical, neck craning up so that beak and tail are parallel. In a while the female will emerge, execute some of her wounded, fluttering rushes, head down, wings spread and trailing. . . . Courtship goes on much longer in birds than is commonly supposed. I lay down the binoculars. I leave them in position and walk quietly to the place where I have left the short-handled pick with which I do my digging, and the plastic bucket I use for conveying away the earth (every particle has to be carried to the secret tip I have established behind the house).

I have felt for quite some time that a subsidiary tunnel would be a splendid idea, to run at an angle of about sixty degrees from the main tunnel and emerge among the beech trees on the other side of the grounds. If I could complete this I should be able to traverse the whole area without once needing to surface. Starting work this morning, this particular morning, after what Audrey said, is an act of faith on my part or perhaps it is simply the need to negate her words. She has told me I must leave within a month; but if I embark on a tunnel that will take at least six months to complete, then obviously I cannot leave in a month. Thus I try to delude myself, knowing all the time how completely in earnest Audrey is.

She knew whose the teeth were of course, even though, when Gravelin had been finally quietened, they were no longer to be found on the plate. I tried at first to insinuate that Gravelin was hallucinated. *Did you look closely at the pupils of her eyes?* But everyone had glimpsed the obscenity. Audrey looked at me in silence, a scrutiny difficult for me to sustain. But why, Simon? Why, tell me, why. No answer. How could I explain the outrageous symmetry of that mousse, that primeval dome, the tribal noises, and the shocks I had received that day, first the boy and then the gardener? A sudden impulse, Audrey, I said, attempting placatory gestures of the hand. But it is madness, Audrey said. Something in her face aroused flickers of compunction, beneath the queenliness assumed for the interview a genuine hurt, a genuine bewilderment. You know how I worry over these supper parties, how I want everything to be just so, you know all this yet you deliberately . . .

I enter my tunnel at the rhododendrons and walk slowly along, flashlight moving from side to side. An earthworm, emerging from the wall, sways its purple trunk slowly back and forth, half of it is still plugged in earth. The light lingers on it briefly, giving it a pinkish transparent radiance, then passes on, leaving the creature writhing in the dark to resolve its dilemma, choose earth or air. I count the paces, stop at the place where I have to begin. Now with considerable misgivings I must take up a section of roof over the main tunnel. I must do this, because it is necessary to stand upright, actually in the trench, while I am digging. It is not very dangerous, since practically the whole of me is still below the ground. But if by chance someone were to enter the grounds very quietly, by some other means than the gate (which cannot be opened soundlessly) and take a diagonal path, pausing frequently to disguise the sounds of his approach, after skirting the pond (apparently lifeless but in reality pullulating), he would come upon me from behind, would see a man, head only above ground, wielding with persistence a hand-pick, his scalp below the sparse hairs on the crown reddening from minute to minute with sun or exertion. To avoid providing such a spectacle is my daily care. To guard against it now I glance continually over my shoulder as I work. Regularly, steadily, I swing the pick up and bring it down. . . .

This house it is finally clear to me is not of dimensions large enough for both of us, Simon. What a frighteningly composed face you had, uttering these words. Like a judge passing sentence, pronouncing for a whole society. *So I am giving you a month.* There was perhaps a point at which the situation could have been saved. A point before the hurt changed into that judge's composure. Perhaps when she began the recounting of past wrongs I could have queried some, turned the interview from arraignment to debate; no Audrey you are wrong, I did not drown the Siamese cat of which Howard was so fond, for example. But I said nothing, merely kept up the gestures of appeasement. Let me remind you, Simon, that you have lived in this house fifteen years free of charge, Howard took you in because you were my brother, for my sake, do you think it was for yours? And the least you could have done out of respect for his memory, was to keep up these grounds of which he was so proud. . . .

Where could I go if I was forced from here? What could I do? Nearly all my little income gone on rent. No privacy, no secrecy, no space. Pedalling off on a bicycle at weekends to watch birds and lovers. All my remaining years spent above ground, in full view. How could I support it?

The sweat runs down my face. I stop for a breather and watch a ladybird climb up the long stem of a grass about six inches from my eyes. It stops half way up and its spotted carapace splits as though wings would be unsheathed, but nothing further happens. Audrey would try to put some humanness into this beetle, she could never let it alone to be alien, vital organs immersed in blood, skeleton on the outside. She would try to attribute qualities that she could understand, because she is always trying to improve an occasion; that was my crime when I dropped the teeth, *I ruined an occasion*. In fact, coming to think of it, Audrey smells of the effort; the scent she uses whether it be gardenia, lily-of-the-valley or violets, designed to suggest whatever blend of timidity and consent, to me has a strenuous odour, the odour of countless enhanced occasions. Perhaps that is why she always overacts so terribly, even in the insignificant roles she has so far been given, she is trying to improve the playwright's occasion for him. . . .

The ladybird joins its wing-cases neatly, resumes its way along the grass. The red ovals on its back are not regular but of various sizes, not clear in outline either but seeming infused. It reaches the end of the stem and stops again. I look up from it at the sky, empty of clouds and birds.

After a little while I resume work, I make five trips, my bucket loaded with earth. As I return for the fifth time, just as I am crossing the drive, I hear the gate, not a loud noise, the dull sound of the metal gate striking the stone kerb at the side of the drive. In two strides, still holding the bucket, I am across the drive, in among the rhododendrons. I sink to my knees and crouch there, waiting for whatever might come up the drive.

The crunch of the gravel. Light rather slow steps. Then

round the first curve of the drive, walking slowly with a pronounced hip roll, a young man whom I have never seen before. For five or six yards, I have a clear view. Short, only about five feet six or seven, and thin. Very dark, something foreign looking about him, his hair jet black and curly and shining with oil. Drawing level now. Surely not more than twenty-one or -two, if that. A sullen face. Passing me now, he looks continually from side to side but his head turns only a fraction. *I know who you are.* I have him for a moment or two in profile, rather Byronic with those curls but without the famous purgative pallor, and with no forehead to speak of, a straight nose and long lashes and a mouth with a very full lower lip, a sulky mouth. I watch his narrow back recede. That swagger and the quiet slow steps, the frequent sidelong glances convey an effect of apprehensive readiness.

The passing of a total stranger along the drive is an unusual thing these days.

I wait for some moments, then make my way to a point from which I can observe the front of the house. I see him emerge from the drive. He goes up the steps of the terrace, knocks at the door, pauses, knocks again. Nobody comes. He takes some paces back, appears undecided. He looks away from the house, towards the grounds, towards where I am standing. Then he glances up at the sky, down again at the lawn. He moves along the terrace towards the steps, then stops again, turns, goes back up to the door and knocks once more. This time it is opened immediately by Marion. They exchange a few words and the young man enters. I stand where I am for five minutes, ten minutes, then very quietly go round to the back of the house and let myself in. Marion is in the kitchen, washing up. She looks up at me vaguely as I enter and smiles in her gentle, really rather rabbity way. I notice not for the first time the hairs on her thin arms, the half inch of petticoat showing beneath her skirt. 'Visitors?' I say, wrinkling my nose at her as though it were something I had detected by smell. 'He's come about the gardening,' Marion says, her smile disappearing.

She turns away from me to go on with the dishes. She is wearing a faded plum-coloured jumper, rather too tight for her, and I notice, again not for the first time, that Marion has very good breasts, small but perfectly shaped. I experience however no desire to dwell upon them, impose on them that isolation always necessary to my enjoyment. I cannot do this with Marion, she is too contiguous, too real, has been ever since the day five years ago when she appeared in the house a white-faced, skinny child with prominent teeth and completely inoffensive eyes, still dazed by the death of her mother. She has grown since then of course, but has come too near to me to be viewed, too much a part of everyday life, with her skimpy clothes, frizzy perms, fugitive gaze.

I leave the kitchen, proceed along the passage and so up to my own room where I wait and listen with the door ajar. After what seems a long time for an interview of this sort, I hear the door of the sitting-room opened, and my sister's voice. I leave my room and take up a position on the second landing of the stairs. Craning my neck I see very briefly the top of the young man's oiled head. He leaves by the back door, the door to which, of course, he should have first applied himself. My sister passes once more into the sitting-room and I am about to turn back to my own room when she reappears, walks a few paces along the passage almost to the foot of the stairs, then stops dead and stands quite still. This is extraordinary be-haviour. If she looked up she might see me but I could pretend to be descending. She does not however look up. Her whole body droops as though with extreme fatigue, and her head is inclined forward. Then, while I watch her in wonder, she straightens herself, raises her head. She lifts her hands to her breasts. She cups her breasts with her hands, remains a moment thus quite still and then with a curiously deliberate gesture, moves her hands down over the breasts and the whole front of her body to the waist.

Josh ...

THEY NEEDED A gardener all right. I could see that from the
start, soon as I got through the gate. You didn't need to be no
mastermind to see that. The drive is gravel a course, nothing
much can happen to that, but you only had to look right or
left to see nettles and stuff waist high, no, what am I saying,
they was at eye level some of them, talk about a jungle. Nothing
been done in there for years. I got a feeling going up the drive
that I was in the wrong shop. I can sense things. I don't know
if it was because it was all overgrown or what. There was
something wrong with the atmosphere like. I could hear myself
walking up the drive and I got this very strange feeling that it
wasn't really solid, like just a crust I was on, like ice or the dry
crust you get over mud sometimes. I felt I had to put my feet
down careful, can't explain it really. I am psychic, after all,
a course. Anyway it never did feel friendly, right from the start
and I get a feeling sometimes as I am moving about the place,
that there is an Unseen Presence. I told this to Mortimer and
he laughed. Mortimer doesn't believe in them sort a things,
atmosphere and that. Mortimer is analytical. I am more the
creative type myself. But I like to tell him and I like him to
laugh, I expect it, and it gives him pleasure, I can tell, being
able to be analytical with me. So it is a good thing all round.
It is one of the ways Mortimer and me go together. Wonder
what he's doing now, chatting them up on the stall I expect.
Getting them in.

I never seen the house till the last minute. I come round a

bend in the drive and there it was, lawn on the left, if you can call it a lawn, and then the house bang in front. Five steps up to what she calls the terrace. Door with a big brass knocker, no bell. And it turns out, only the two of them live in it, the brother and sister. Marion too, a course. That is a funny thing, I don't think of Marion living in the house, not in the same way. She does not seem to take up much space like, maybe that's it. She moves about the place but she don't take up much room. She is a bit on the thin side. I like them thin. I can't stand fat. Sometimes I am walking along behind a woman, I am looking at her legs, every time she puts her foot down her fat leg wobbles, that is disgusting in my opinion. Why don't they go on a diet? Or there is massage. Men's legs don't do that. I know which is Marion's bedroom.

I haven't told Mortimer about Marion yet. I will have to sooner or later, a course, but I don't feel like it just now. He will go on at me, soon as I tell him, specially since I did not mention it to begin with. Mortimer sees deep into things, he talks things over and a lot of stuff comes out that you never realised before. And what he comes out with might be bad for Marion. It might make me see her in a different light. I would rather have just my own idea of her for the time being. It is not doing anything against Mortimer, because I am going to tell him.

I like her. I like her being thin and her face, well she isn't what you'd call pretty but she's got nice eyes and a nice skin and she has got good tits even if she is thin, they showed up in that pink pullover like Jaffas, well tangerines, wonder how old she is, seventeen?

Only three of them in the house (two, I told Mortimer). Doesn't seem right. What do they want with such a big house? That is exactly the question Mortimer asked when I told him. He always puts his finger on it. There are people living at this moment, at this very moment, he said, in compounds and camps, living in tents, kids born in tents, refugees. It makes you think, he said. Well, I agree, a course, it doesn't seem right. In this day and age.

I went up on to the terrace and knocked at the door. I knocked and waited, knocked again. No one came. I didn't hear no movements inside the house. Nothing at all. Well, it gave me a funny feeling, a big house like that. What I mean is, you'd expect people about. I might have turned round and gone back there and then. What if I'd of just turned round and walked away? There would of been no Marion. I looked back the way I came. You couldn't see nothing much of the drive from there, only the big dusty bushes where the drive began and across the lawn more bushes and some trees, you couldn't see nothing, just trees and leaves and everything quiet. No wind, nothing moving that you could *see*, but there was this feeling of movement inside it all, I dunno, a sort of swarming as you might say, but no noise with it and nothing you could see. I might of gone away there and then, I didn't like it, but I knocked one more time and they opened the door. Marion did. Not that I knew her name then. I only found out her name this morning. Met her behind the house while I was getting out the scythe. Smiled at me, she did. White cotton dress on. Are you managing all right? she says. Teeth stick out a bit, buck teeth really, but I don't mind them. Yes, I said. Yes, thank you very much. And then, before we can get talking, there is this sort of la-di-da scream from somewhere at the side of the house, *Mario—o—on, where are yo—o—ou?* So that is your name, I said. Yes, she says, what is yours? Josiah. That is an unusual name isn't it? Then that screech again, *Mario—o—on.* I better go, she says. Funny girl with that dress, frizzy hair, big brown eyes. She don't take enough trouble over her appearance. She don't make the best of herself. She ought to grow her hair out to begin with and use a bit a make-up. One of these days I'll tell her.

It's wonderful really. I am sitting here now against this tree. Sun on my legs. Smell of the cut grass. Thinking about Marion and her funny smile and Mrs Wilcox all in blue. Pale-blue twin set and a dark-blue skirt. I notice colours, always have done.

She must like blue because the sofa and armchairs in the room where I waited were covered with little blue flowers like forget-me-nots or something of that sort, made a nice pattern, very artistic, and a low round table with a copper vase on it but nothing in the vase. Not enough colour in that room, nothing to draw the eye as you might say. I would of had something in a bit brighter myself, some gay cushion covers like, not that it wasn't tasteful. I said to Mortimer, you have to have a centrepiece otherwise you don't get no grouping, there wasn't no centrepiece in that room. I like to show him I know something about décor. That is your province, Josiah, he said to me. I have always been interested in it. If I see one of them magazines lying about I always look at the pictures of interiors. I don't bother with the words underneath, usually. We was always moving about when I was little. Reading is hard work for me as a matter a fact, but I never say nothing to him about that.

Only thing on her not blue was her necklace, that was pearls, but I dunno if they was real. I got up soon as she come through the door, all the time I was sitting there waiting I was reminding myself to do that when she come in. I know my manners. She was about the same height as me. Face very pale and *small*, with these straight eyebrows and a sharp straight nose. She looked pleased with herself. And this grey hair like. You have come from the Labour Exchange, have you? In a manner of speaking, I said. I was still thinking how peculiar the place was and how I come to be there. I wasn't sure at that moment that the Labour had anything to do with it. That might sound funny, but there it is. She opened her eyes a bit. Bossy eyes. What on earth does that mean? she says. Very la-di-da, a course. A man either comes from a Labour Exchange or he doesn't, she says. I saw the red light right there. Yes, I said. They sent me. You look very young, she says. Have you had experience of gardening? Well, I said, I done a bit, I said, but I understood it was odd jobs. Then she asked me how old I was. She should not of done, Mortimer said. She should not of asked that. It lay outside her province, Mortimer said. Positively feudal, he said, and I am giving his own words now. It is a wonder, he said, she didn't prise your jaw open and have a dekko at your molars. No, quite unacceptable, he said. It is from that moment that I date his taking against Mrs Wilcox. He wouldn't hear nothing good of her after that. You have got no pride, Josiah, he said, but it didn't mean nothing to me. I am twenty, I said. Then there was a bit of a silence and I looked at her face. She has the sort of face you can't tell if she is smiling or not. It is very young, she says. In time, I says, I'll be older. Quick, just like that, I come out with it. It was one of the first things I told Mortimer, how I come out with that, but he didn't seem to think much of it. I thought he would of laughed. I never understand what makes Mortimer laugh, he's got a sense of humour all of his own. He laughed when I told him how I stood up when she first come in, he laughed at that, I dunno why, he don't like to share a joke. You can ask him, he won't tell you, just go on laughing. I could not do that, myself. When he laughs his lower lip draws right back showing the bottom gums, his eyes close nearly. Mortimer does not usually make any noise when he laughs.

Wish she was here now. Marion I mean, not Mrs Wilcox, Christ. Sitting here beside me on the grass. Just talking like, not doing nothing. Or maybe she lies down on her back, moves her legs a bit just by accident like. She's showing her legs but she don't know it. She has got her eyes closed all the time. I can see right up her legs but she don't know it. No, wait a bit, she knows it all the time like, but she don't let on, she is doing it on purpose. I put my hand up her skirt and she still keeps her eyes closed. . . .

Simon ...

STRAIGHTENING MYSELF I look once more across the quiet green field at the bungalow: nothing moves there except three white hens at the side. My binoculars rest ready focused in their niche in the hedge. Today is Monday, washing day. I never willingly miss a washing day at the bungalow, mainly because of the few minutes while she is hanging out the clothes —a time when sops to decorum are often not paid. For instance her hair may well be escaping from the insufficient pins, her skirt unzipped showing a gaudier seam. She is a woman of generous proportions, and in the warmth and steam and exertion of washing, those proportions are more likely to escape confinement. I have known her large breasts swing untrammelled, beneath a flimsy blouse. Once I got her against the sun, not apparently wearing anything under a cotton skirt. (On that occasion I became over excited and vomited.) She is a careless woman, I thank God.

This morning, however, I cannot enjoy my usual feelings of anticipation. I am troubled by the gardener's presence in the grounds and by Audrey's vindictiveness towards me which shows no sign of lessening. (Only yesterday evening she asked me, when we met on the stairs, whether I had yet found somewhere else to live.) And with such composure, such absence of heat: I don't think I showed her my fear however. I know all the time I am standing here that there is something I positively must do this morning, a job that takes priority over everything else and that is I must erase all signs of the tributary tunnel I was rash enough to begin last week. Absurd to think I should be able to do any tunnelling with that gardener about. He is here now, today, he is round at the side of the house, weeding between the flags of the paved courtyard that Audrey says she wants to turn into a *patio*. A word she would not have used before joining the Dramatic Society. All last week, under her direction, he was cutting the lawn, rooting up the dock and dandelion, getting things ready for the garden party which will be held in the grounds with the object of raising funds for the Dramatic Society. Audrey herself has been very energetic since the gardener started work here, getting up at eight and walking round the place in corduroy trousers. . . . The weeding should take him all morning but one never knows when he might start poking about in the shrubbery, come upon a half-dug trench, the earth still raw, follow it up, discover the main tunnel, the whole thing. All my work . . . I couldn't allow that to happen. I must fill it in again, cover all traces. Then I shall have time to watch, safeguard myself, form a plan. . . .

Still, however, undecided, I look beyond the bungalow at the green wheat. About a foot high now, quite still today. I remember the field ploughed black in the windy days of March and the lapwings overhead and the way they seemed to die in the air. Sweep down on the wind, check, somehow, for a second, fold their wings and drop like a stone, then at the last moment, recover, beat upwards, uttering always at the point of recovery a distraught cry of joy, that's the only word for it, this abandonment must be happiness in the bird, what else? Strange that this intensest moment should bear for the human observer a resemblance to death. . . .

I remember the tall gold wheat of August stiff as brocade in the windless air in the fields along the river bank. We walked along the river bank, the three of us, till we reached the big meander; wheat and larks and poppies. Deep still water, a little shingled border on the near side. We changed very modestly behind bushes and then we swam and afterwards lay

down on the shingle, Audrey's friend in the middle. It was such
a hot day. A boy's costume, high in the body but narrow
fronted and with narrow shoulder straps, I can remember every
detail of that costume now after all these years, the exact width
of the straps is reproduced in my mind, and the high front
going up almost to the neck but very narrow. Perhaps it was her
brother's. Wrinkling as it dried and loosening from her body.
She was a very thin girl, painfully thin as they say, and white-
skinned, very white she looked in that black bathing suit which
had been designed for a boy, and which in drying wrinkled
back, loosened, and revealed her left breast to me. The sun on
my eyelids and a skein of light between eyes and lids. Hot
shingle, texture of the pebbles, heat flowing over me, all
seeming now like heralding sensations, a light massage of the
senses—preliminary to the moment when, in a sun stupor,
turning my head and half opening my eyes, I saw at a distance
of some eighteen inches with a sort of nimbussed radiance,
the nude slope of my sister's friend's left breast up to and
decidedly including the nipple. The temporary and provisional
nature of the vision was what impressed me first, the need for a
devoted stillness on my part. Even my breathing I stilled,
staring closely at the slightly freckled white skin of the slope
which rose to the first isolated pimples, freckles as it were in
relief, milk-chocolate brown in colour; the nipple itself not
quite perfect in shape and irregular in texture, the colour of a
healing bruise, the tip redder with its suffusion of blood. A
tender little dip, a declivity, at the very peak, as if the nipple,
urged up by some gentle insistence of the blood, or raised from
the malleable teat by some divine inhalation, had then subsided,
ever so slightly caved in. My sister's friend's nipple had thus
the look of perfection slightly marred.

A cool breeze blew over the water and I watched the flesh
round the nipple pimple more prominently, the roseate cor-
rugations become more sharply defined. She did not know, of
course, either that the breeze had produced these changes in the
appearance of her left breast or that I was busily and, in spite

of my excitement, competently recording them; and this serenity of her ignorance was maintained beyond my endurance, caused me finally to turn from her on to my other side, knees drawn up and body arched, foetal in convulsions. No one can understand who has not experienced it how almost overwhelming such throes can be when induced by the intensities of sight alone, how the whole being is flooded, almost borne away. . . . And when I opened my eyes again there was the staring wheat. . . .

Still nothing happening at the bungalow. I can wait no longer, that trench must be attended to. I begin to make my way through the grounds. It is a beautiful morning, earlier it rained a little and now there is what seems a delicate transparent sheath over everything. Somewhere on my left a blackbird is singing. I skirt the pond which with the advent of summer has become distinctly malodorous, hearing as I do so three plops of frogs. A little beyond this I enter the area of shrubbery and go directly to my so recently begun trench. The only safe way, as I see immediately, is to fill it up with earth again and cover it over with grass sods. But the earth will have to be brought back from the tip behind the house, a laborious business.

I stand for some moments confronting the need to begin work. I remind myself that it is a very urgent matter. Audrey might at any moment, striding about in her corduroy trousers, order the gardener to divest of vegetation Howard's seat and trellis and arbour, not a dozen yards from where I stand. In that case discovery would be inevitable. At the moment these things are hardly recognisable. The rustic bench is so invaded by grass that it looks like some weirdly shaped boat trapped in weed. Beyond it Howard built a rose arbour and a trellised walk, training various creepers to grow over it, clematis and the like, and, of course, the cottage roses, which still multitudinously bloom. However, ruder plants have clambered for years unchecked over trellis and arbour, making of the whole a rather monstrous hump of accreted vegetation, closing both

ends in a tangled mass of honeysuckle and bindweed and
bryony so that only the smaller and more active quadrupeds
could now gain admittance to the wooden table inside, over
which poor Howard must have envisaged his *fêtes champêtres*.

Still deferring the job of filling up the trench I gaze fixedly
at the roses, great sprays of them deep pink and sweetly
scented, the petals rucked and folded and intricate. Their
weight pulls the sprays down, very graceful and elegaic. I walk
across with a sudden feeling of unhappiness, and pick one of
the unopened roses. It is cool, very slightly moist. I open the bud,
folding back the petals, which soften and become pliable
immediately from the warmth of my fingers, betraying thus
the degenerate stock. In the heart of the flower, the petals are
almost white, with only the faintest of flushes. With surprise
and disapproval I discern numbers of tiny gleaming beetles
scurrying about. Even in the interior of a rose it seems, there
is no inviolate space.

Suddenly, still holding the rose, I hear a swishing or hissing
sound of very brief duration from somewhere in front of me in
the area adjoining the road. It is repeated almost immediately
and thereafter at intervals of about five seconds. An alien sound,
quite distinct from all others in the grounds, distinct precisely
because I cannot identify it, it comes clear to my ears with the
effect of a harsh, possibly minatory respiration; it would
appear to be coming from the open area between the hedge and
the shrubbery.

I move cautiously forward towards the sound. Passing from
the cover of the trees into the shrubbery I am obliged at first
to crouch and then to go on hands and knees. The sound
grows steadily clearer, no longer like a breath, however harsh,
but now with a composite sound as of many minute collisions.
Then I see him, fifty or sixty yards away, standing in the open
not far from the hedge, his body turning, hands held low, the
scythe audibly slicing through the grass, nettle, buttercup,
foxglove. The sun catches the long blade as it is drawn back,
shreds of green adhere to it. He stands with head slightly

lowered, his oiled curls shining in the sun as though listening carefully himself to the hiss of the blade. I note that he has taken off his jacket but not rolled up his sleeves which are long and cover part of his hands and this seems to me in its inappropriate elegance entirely characteristic of him.

It occurs to me that I could speak to him now. I could warn him for example to keep away from the robin's nest, which has eggs in it. I could go back through the shrubbery to the drive then walk boldly up it and accost the gardener in confident loud tones. I could establish a relationship with the gardener. I do none of these things, however, and in fact the next moment the opportunity is gone because I hear steps on the drive to my right, quite close, not more than a dozen yards away, very light steps, otherwise I should have heard them before. Before I have time to do more than crouch a little lower, I see the upper part of Audrey passing down the drive, carrying a copper tray with tea things on it. On her face there is a strange expression, a look of tension which is not, however, unhappy, almost as though she is suppressing a desire to laugh, suppressing all evidence of the desire. On the tray I glimpse jug, bowl, teapot, even a plate of biscuits. She is wearing a pink mohair jumper, short-sleeved, which I had not known formed part of her wardrobe. It looks astoundingly frivolous.

She disappears from view along the drive. A minute or two later, however, I see her entering the clearing where the gardener is working. He grounds his scythe, straightens up and turns towards the right. She approaches him, bearing the tray. She appears to hesitate for a moment, then lays it down carefully on the ground between them. It is too far for me to hear what is said. They stand together there, she with hands clasped before her and head up high, he, too, unusually braced-looking, almost soldierly with his hands down at his sides.

Then she turns away, disappears again, apparently making her way back to the house. Quickly I crawl over to slightly better cover. I hear her steps passing along the drive but I do not look up. When I look towards the hedge again the gardener is not visible. Presumably he is sitting down somewhere having his tea. I extricate myself with care from the bushes, going on hands and knees until I feel quite safe from detection, then quickly make my way to the far corner of the grounds where I left my binoculars. I do not, however, return to my former position but very cautiously advance to the border of the drive, cross it on tip-toe and, kneeling behind one of the rhododendrons, I look through the leaves to get my bearings. I can see nothing of the gardener from here. I edge along towards the hedge, keeping well within the cover of the bushes bordering the drive. Heat and exertion combine to affect my breathing. I glance continually through the rhododendron leaves. A certain hysterical anxiety is beginning to possess me when at last I see him, at a distance of about seventy yards, sitting with his back against the first of the birches. His head is lowered in what I at first take to be sleep, but then I see that there is something in his hands. I experience as always, some difficulty in focusing, but at last he is clear in every detail, the shiny curls low on his forehead, the long lashes, the full mouth hanging very slightly open, thin brown cherishing fingers. But I cannot make out what thing he is holding. It lies in the palm of his left hand, a curved piece of it projecting beyond the fingers rather like a single claw. His right hand holds a small knife with which he is regularly scraping the object as though scraping a carrot. My own hands begin to tremble with the weight of the binoculars. It is something he is cutting.

Flies have discovered my person and found it beguiling. Just when I think I can bear it no longer, the caressing motion of the right hand, the hand with the knife, stops, and the hand falls away. The left hand is moved forward and upward, the object between thumb and middle finger held up before the gardener's face, turned now this way, now that. It is a little wooden horse.

Josh . . .

THIS TIME I will give it to him. When it is finished a course, it is not finished yet. Won't be long, mind. I got the head right, no need to touch that again. Horses' heads isn't easy, all bone, can't mess about with bone, you got to get it right. I ought to know what horses look like, with my dad in the carting business. When it is finished I will give it to him. I think I will. I said the same about other things I done but in the end I never did it. I never gave them to nobody. I think I will give him the horse though. I never gave him nothing before. Trouble is, I dunno how he would take it. That is what is holding me back. He might laugh and what would I do then? Giving people things might not be what he is used to. You never know with Mortimer. He is different to other people. You never know what he'll do. The other thing is that I don't know how to do it, I mean actually hand it over. I would have to say something. Please accept this small gift which I done myself. I can't see myself saying that, not with him looking at me all the time. He don't even know I can carve things, I never told him. Anyway it is not finished yet, wait till it is finished.

Maybe if it come as a surprise like, it would be easier. Say me and Mortimer have left this place, say we are on the road. He's packed up the job on the stall and I have packed up here and we are on the road. Travelling light, plenty lolly for fags, mugs a tea. One of them dual carriageways, bright green grass down the middle, blue asphalt with fresh white lines and sloping, a long slope up behind us. You can look back at the lines of traffic. The cars come along fast, pass us with just a hiss like, but if you look behind up the slope you can see the lines of them in the sunshine, in the distance they seem to be moving very slow. And they are not separate but the sunshine joins them all together, like melting, the light on the windows and chassis. Right at the top of the slope they are not moving at all, just all melted together and shining. Funny how clear I can see them cars. Mortimer is dressed in navy-blue slacks and a camel-hair jacket, double-breasted, and I am in my orange shirt and my safari slacks, pale-blue linen. We have just got down from the cab of a lorry at a big green roundabout where the roads all go different ways. We can go down any of them, any one we like. Across the road there is this little café and there is music coming from inside, a man's voice singing. Mortimer and me smile at each other like, standing there all by ourselves at the roundabout and I put my hand in my pocket and take out the horse and give it to him, this is for you Mortimer, no wait a minute I don't say nothing and Mortimer don't say nothing for a bit, just goes on smiling, no that's not right, he stops smiling because he is so impressed. Did you really carve this yourself, Josiah? I had no idea. . . .

Must be about eleven, better get back to work. Any rate I can *cut* now with this scythe. When I started off it would not of gone through butter. I couldn't get on at all, I had to go and ask for something to sharpen it with. I went through the trees and I come out at the lawn facing the terrace. Mrs Wilcox was sitting up on the terrace in a deck chair. She was wearing dark glasses and looking at a magazine. She didn't see me, well I don't think she did, till I was at the top of the steps and starting to walk towards her. Then she looked up. Her skirt was up over her knees and her legs was parted a bit but she didn't make no move to cover them up. She just watched me coming, with the sun shining on her dark glasses. It didn't matter about me, a course. Well, she said, what is it? She hasn't got bad legs for a woman her age. I need a whetstone or something, I said. Something to sharpen the scythe with. A whetstone? she said.

I know nothing about whetstones. Can't you manage without one? She said this as if she thought I was making a fuss about nothing. And she moved her knees together. Well, you see, I said, the scythe is blunt. It is not cutting. She had on this sort of sun dress, square cut and low at the neck with these very narrow straps over the shoulders. Her arms and shoulders was not fat exactly—she is not a fat woman Mrs Wilcox—but sort of puffy, not firm, and they was a bit raw-looking with the sun. There will probably be something of the sort in the shed behind, she said. You can go and look there if you like. Oh, no, wait a minute, she said. It is kept locked. The keys are hanging up in the kitchen. Go and ask Marion. Well, that would of suited me down to the ground but before I could move she said, Oh dear I forgot, Marion is out shopping, I suppose I shall have to go myself.

She started trying to get up but the funny thing was that she couldn't. Well, she could of got up easy enough if there hadn't of been anyone watching. The deck chair was let down low so her bottom was only an inch or two from the ground and her legs was much higher. She tried for a bit but there was nothing to push herself against like so she had to turn sideways, get her legs over the wooden frame of the chair and that nearly brought the chair over, she had to spread her legs like, for balance, and that gave me a view of her red knickers. Red knickers, I would not of associated Mrs Wilcox with red knickers. She went on working at it, it was like watching a beetle that can't get turned right side up. I come a bit closer and got hold of her arm. I closed my hand round her arm high up. I felt my fingers sink in like, she was spongy up there near the armpit. Her skin was hot from the sun. I kept on pulling till she was on her feet. It's quite all right, she said, very snappish like, and she pulled her arm away almost before she was standing. She did not like being hauled up like a sack, a course. All the same, it was the day after that she started coming with tea in the morning. I mean, she could always make Marion do that, if she didn't want to herself. I got the scythe sharpened anyway.

Wonder what they are doing now on the stall. Albert will be going on about that girl he got in the family way. With his cross-eyes. *Every night for a bloody month I shagged her, wouldn't you of done?* Good job for Albert it was dark, she probably never did get a good look at him. And old Mrs Morris, counting the shots. *Look at him working the rock, that's what I call grafting.* Her dozy old head wobbling all the time. Can't say I am sorry to be off that stall. Except for Mortimer, a course. I must say I miss working alongside Mortimer and getting the benefit of his conversation. Now it's the height of the season like, he's working there till nine or ten every night, I don't get so much chance to see him. Wonder who they got on the stall instead of me. Mortimer never said. They are certain to have somebody by now. I don't suppose him and Mortimer will have much in common. He told me himself that he don't have time for nobody on the stall but me. You are not a typical stall attendant, Josiah, he said to me. His own words. This new chap will be just a typical stall attendant.

He must of seen something in me that first time. One month and three days ago. Else why should he of bothered to save me from getting bashed up? He might easy of been bashed up himself. It was a Tuesday night, the night after I got here. (I was in Harrogate all winter, working in the Grand, in the kitchens.) I didn't know nobody. I went into this pub for a shandy. I don't know the name of it, not even yet. I never went back there. Shandy, I said to the girl behind the bar. Give me a pint of shandy please. I always drink a shandy when I am thirsty. Soon as I said it I felt this bloke staring at me, this bloke standing at the bar, he started staring soon as I said shandy. But I didn't look. I mean, there are blokes who will stare at you in pubs. I don't remember anyone else at the bar but this one bloke, it being a weeknight, and still early, there might of been a few people sitting down, but I didn't have no time to notice, because this bloke got hold of my arm, tight hold and hurting. When I looked round, there's this big red face with little pig eyes, getting up close to me. What's wrong wid you, he says, an Irish bastard, drunk he was, and I knew he was going to hit me any minute. That's not a Christian drink, he says. What kind of a drink is that? It is a Jew drink, he says. You must be a Jew, he says. I couldn't feel my arm at all, it was numb. He was squeezing, then letting go a bit, then squeezing again and his bloodshot eyes and all, I just lost my presence of mind like, if he hadn't of been holding me I think I would of fallen, my legs was like jelly. I could feel that big fist of his crunching on my nose. It was not just that he was Irish, and everyone knows it's a word and a blow with them, but this bloke was off his head. He wasn't even looking at me. Now then, the girl behind the bar said, Give over, she said. He is a bleeding Jew, the bloke said. You watch your language, she said. I couldn't think of nothing to say, just looked into his little blue eyes and they wasn't seeing me, they was looking far away, and his hand kept on squeezing and loosening as if he was milking a cow. Please, I said. Please, mister. My voice sounded like somebody else's.

Then Mortimer was there, right beside me, I didn't know then who it was, a course, just this tall pale fellow, very well dressed, navy-blue suit, maroon tie. What are you doing with this boy? he says. Don't you know this is an Irish boy? He is a bleeding Jew, the Mick says, but he started sort of looking at me and after a bit he took his hand off my arm. He come in here, he said, he come in here, bold as brass, asking for a shandy, what kind of drink is that? I spoke to him civil and he told me to get stuffed. (That was a lie, a course, I never said nothing to him from start to finish.) He may be dark-complexioned, Mortimer said, but his name is Murphy. Mine is Milligan. Will you have a pint on me? He jerked his head at me and I got out, round the bar and out to the Gents at the back. I stayed there a bit, I still couldn't feel my arm and I thought I was going to be sick. I went into the W.C. and sat for a bit on the seat, till I felt better. I nearly didn't go back, though. I nearly didn't go back there at all. I could of gone through the yard and out to the street without going back in there. I dunno to this day why I went back but it turned out to be the best thing I ever done because that is how Mortimer and me become friends.

The Irish bloke was still there but he didn't take no notice of me. He had his nose in another pint. Mortimer and me sat at one of the tables and we got talking. He wouldn't let me thank him. I could tell from the start he was educated like. He had this flow of words and he could talk on any subject. He had been in Penzance up to a fortnight before, working in the dry dock, painting hulls. He had got fed up with that and moved on here and he had got a job on a rifle range in the Pleasure Park down on the front. He told me they still needed someone and that was how I got on to the job. I wish we could of had the same digs but there was no room in his. I had a job to find a place and then I have to share a bed with this bloke who does the Fairy Lights, well it isn't good enough, not for three pound ten a week. (He is a professional man, mind you, he is a qualified engineer.)

I will never forget how Mortimer saved me from getting bashed up. That bloke wasn't right in the head, apart from being Irish—and that is another lot that ought to be in the compounds. He could of disfigured me for life or any rate till I could save up for the Plastic Surgery.

This time I am going to give him it. I will watch his face and if he is going to start laughing, I will turn round and walk away. Why is giving him it so difficult? He is the one that I want to have it.

Simon ...

SHE IS WEARING a red dress this morning, a sleeveless red dress. She picks off the blown roses from the bush beside the bungalow. When she extends her plump arms, arching them delicately over the bush to avoid the thorns, I see her dark armpits, I see a silky edge through the sleeve hole of her undergarment, I see the tremor of muscle in her upper arm when she tightens her fingers to squeeze off the roses. I experience a faint nausea, willing her with all the force at my command to continue this series of movements, to submit herself rather to this pattern which has been imposed on her, part of the divine plan, because whatever meaning she is inventing in her finite mind for her present actions and whatever agitation is set up in my finite loins, our wills have nothing to do with it, we are all grounded in being and the roses are simply a pretext whatever she may suppose; what is she supposing now as she bends farther and farther forward reaching with delicately angled arm, her fleshy white legs pressed close together, not bending at the knee, whatever it is she cannot wriggle off the impalement of my regard, don't move, please don't move, just for a minute. . . . Damn! She has seen something farther down the field, something invisible to me. She straightens herself, looks for some moments across the field, then, apparently deciding the roses need no more attention, she steps back, turns and walks rather slowly back into the house. I am left with feelings of nausea, desolation, and testicular malaise.

What can she have seen? Something of distinctly limited
interest obviously, since it did not occupy her for long. Crane
as I may I cannot see from here, but a few yards down towards
the house the hedge is lower. I am surprised to see Marion at
the far end of the field, walking very slowly through the deep
grass about twenty yards from the hedge, coming in this
direction. But why is she in the field at all, why on that side of
the hedge? She is walking very slowly, looking at the ground
before her, has she perhaps lost something? For these few
moments, as she continues to walk very slowly towards me,
because of the slope of the field behind her and because of the
particular angle of my vision, Marion is set against a background
of horizontal zones as exactly demarcated as those of a tricolour
flag, first the yellow and green dazzle of the sunlit meadow on
which she is walking, then from waist to neck the vivid uniform
green of the young wheat, and her head finally against the
milky blue morning sky. Her isolation makes her seem for the
moment archetypal.

At this point for some reason she goes nearer to the hedge
and so my sight of her is shut off by the line of the hedge itself.
I remain in the same posture for several minutes longer, but
Marion does not re-appear. If she had continued walking she
must surely have come up to me before this. Therefore she
must have either stopped at some point along the hedge or
gone back the way she came, keeping on the return journey
much closer to the hedge and thus remaining invisible to me.
Certainly she could not have struck out across the field without
being seen. Nor was it likely that she had entered the grounds
at any point along the way, since the hedge is five feet high at
least and quite thick. It was of course conceivable that she was
simply out for a walk, taking a bit of exercise, a thing that
people do all the time as I am fully aware. But this explanation
did not satisfy me because I had never known Marion to go
in for such constitutionals before and because of the somewhat
skulking way she had kept to the hedge: people set on walking
strike out boldly, in my experience.

Leaving my post in the corner I began to walk as circumspectly as possible along the inside of the hedge towards the point where, as far as I could judge, Marion had disappeared from view. It did not occur to me at the time to wonder at my actions, indeed it seemed quite natural to spy on Marion in this way; not until considerably later did I realise that this morning had marked a turning point.

I had no desire to become involved in these people's lives, any more than I wanted to involve my teeth in their mousse, that whole summer of spying on people and conjecturing was a nightmare from beginning to end, keeping me from my tunnelling, keeping me from possibly quintessential aspects of the bungalow woman. Audrey forced it on me. It was she who engaged a gardener to poke about in the grounds, distressing me so that I behaved foolishly in the matter of the teeth; she who then proceeded to give me a month's notice to leave. That threat produced the nightmarish talent for detection I now began to show, on the same principle, I suppose, that some creatures, in the proximity of their enemies, emit an offensive odour. . . .

I was right, of course. Even before I heard their voices, heard Marion's voice raised in a laugh, I knew I was right. I stopped immediately. If I had advanced any further I should almost certainly have been seen or heard. There wasn't a great deal of cover immediately adjoining the hedge. I had to make a roughly semicircular detour through the thicker vegetation. I was perspiring and my heart was beating heavily when I heard Marion laugh again, quite clear and close and a moment or two later, body full length and pressed against the ground, peering with utmost caution, I saw him standing with his back to me at the hedge talking over it to somebody who could only be Marion, although I could not see her.

He was standing erect and rather proud-looking, with his hands on his narrow hips and his feet planted a little apart. I could not distinguish any words but again I heard her laugh; obviously the gardener was a gayer fellow than his outward

appearance suggested. The hedge stood between them, like
the sword of old. How long had this been going on? There was
what seemed an ease, an absence of constraint in the conversation, which marked it as not the first. On the other hand they
were not meeting by appointment, that much was clear from
Marion's behaviour earlier. She had known, obviously, that the
gardener was to be found working at this section of the hedge
this morning. She could not have approached him from within
the grounds, picking her way deviously through the undergrowth, because this would have indicated too clearly her
design, removed all pretence of the accidental. So she had
wandered along on the other side of the hedge, perhaps on a
pretext of looking for mushrooms, something of that sort.
Probably she had allowed him to notice her first. . . . I had
not thought Marion capable of so much guile.

I could not help feeling as I lay there, my heart beat returning
to normal and my agitation subsiding, that I was witnessing
something of great, though not yet clearly defined importance,
something portentous for the future; and this sense of signi-
ficance, like a meaning suddenly perceived in something previously obscure, brought with it a momentary lessening of
interest, of concentration—I allowed my attention to be taken
up by a stirring in the grass immediately before my eyes.
Probing a little into the pale roots, I found a huge beautiful
beetle with an iridescent back. A beautiful creature somewhat
distraught now with fear of me. With my forefinger I rolled
him over on to his back; hairy jointed legs waved at me—in
expostulation presumably; the works of the creature were
black and ingenious-looking like clockwork. . . .

I was alerted by the sound of steps through the grass, not far
from me. Looking up I saw that there was no one now at the
hedge. It was the gardener then, making those sounds, since
they were definitely on my side. He was heading, as far as I
tould judge, inwards at right-angles to the hedge. If this was so
I should have him in full view for a few seconds when he had
passed through the laurels adjoining the drive on that side.

Sure enough he emerged, looking as sullen as ever—this dalliance had effected no slightest change in his expression. What was visible of his in any case negligible forehead was strangely smooth, smooth as plaster beneath the curls. For all its permanent sombreness of expression, the gardener's is a face that never seems to have needed to express any but the most unexacting of emotions. He is very young, of course, one mustn't forget that.

I hesitated for some moments, then followed. I had more or less decided to assay the gardener and so was proceeding with something less than my usual care, with the result that I very nearly blundered into Audrey as she came down the drive. Only the fact that she was absorbed in balancing the tea tray saved me from being seen. She looked graver than on the last occasion and was wearing a white blouse with a frilly front.

I stood where I was, waiting for Audrey to return. She took longer than before. I thought she must be chatting to the gardener while he had his tea. At last, when I was beginning to wonder if she had returned to the house by another way, she reappeared without the tray, walking with what seemed a rather spurious briskness, her head up, as if to demonstrate the normality of her whole proceeding. I gave her plenty of time to regain the house, then I made my way to the point where I had seen him scything. He was not there, but after another minute I saw him sitting with his back to one of the birches, studiously whittling away at what I guessed to be the horse. He did not look up though he must have heard me approach. He sat, head studiously bent, outstretched legs in the sun, the rest of him in shadow. Only his hands moved. It occurred to me that for a person who had just had a half-hour tea break, he was being a bit leisurely about resuming work. Moderating my gait to what I hoped was a saunter, I moved towards him. He saw nothing of my saunter, however, as he still did not look up. Even when I stopped before him, raising my hand in a gesture of salutation and smiling broadly, even then he did not look up, and my arm remained suspended rather I felt now in benediction, the smile

losing much of its breadth. For some reason it did not immediately occur to me to speak. I had begun, and almost completed in
fact, the lowering of my arm when he did raise his eyes, so
what he must have seen was a quite pointless motion, a light
slapping of the hand against the thigh. The mere greeting, the
initial contact was proving so difficult a hurdle that I began to
feel agitated and it was very fortunate that at this point I
remembered the device of speech and said, 'Good-morning,
beautiful morning isn't it,' inclining my head towards his
muttered reply. 'No,' I said, 'don't get up,' and fortunately
he did not persist in scrambling to his feet, which would have
obliged us to exchange civilities, but lowered his head once more
to the work that was engaging him. So I had time to collect
myself and also to get a good look at the horse. It was to my
surprise an extremely accomplished piece of carving in sand-
coloured wood, pine perhaps. He had arrested the horse at a
noble moment—distended nostrils, arched neck, heraldic mane.
He held the knife lightly, blade at a little more than right-angles
to the direction of the cut, defining repeatedly the long beautiful
line from belly up towards haunches, again and again, slowly,
his rather dirty thumb pressed against the flattened edge,
guiding the track of the blade, spilling each time a minute
shaving.

'That is a very finely carved horse if I may say so.'

He looked up again, this time more lingeringly. He had blue
eyes of an astounding beauty and vacuity. Looking at those
eyes one understood that the sullen, rather bitter melancholy
of the whole face was merely an accident of bone structure, not
an expression of temperament. 'I done a good few,' he said.
'One time and another.'

'Always horses?'

'Horses, dogs, cats. I done elephants before now.'

'You must be very fond of animals.' He returned no answer
to this, merely continued to look at me—steadily but without
any apparent expectation of more words being said or needed.
He seemed in a way like an animal himself, quiescent, incurious

because the immediate experience was not within the zone of his instinctive life. 'Well,' I said, sketching a gesture in the air before me—a reassuring gesture, but for my reassurance, not his—'Well, there was one thing I wanted to speak to you about, actually, and that was my *hide*, yes you may come across a hide in the course of your scything. Are you interested in birds at all? No perhaps not. What I want you to do is to avoid with your scythe the grass between the hedge and the shrubbery for a dozen yards or so, I could show you where, because I have constructed a *hide* there. . . .' It was no use, of course, I was not conveying anything. I experienced a momentary bafflement and then I had another idea: 'Snakes,' I said. 'Moreover there are small but deadly snakes in that area of the shrubbery, nowhere else in the grounds, there is something nourishing to them in the soil . . . keep out of that area is my advice to you.'

He was staring fixedly at me now. His eyes seemed somewhat more alert, 'Snakes,' he said. 'Nobody said nothing to me about snakes before.'

'Yes indeed,' I said. 'So long as you keep out of the shrubbery you're all right. Don't mention this to my sister, Mrs Wilcox, by the way.'

Suddenly, in making this reference to Audrey, I remembered the pink mohair, the tea tray, that strange look of suppressed mirth, the braced and extrovert walk back along the drive. An idea of a different sort came to me, and without pausing to think I asked the gardener what he did with the horses. 'What do you do with them when they are finished?' I asked him, and he replied with an almost startling promptness and eagerness.

'I was thinking of giving this one away,' he said. 'There's someone I want to have it like, but these things isn't always welcome, that's what it is, Mortimer isn't like other people, you don't know how he'll take things—'

'Give it to my sister,' I said. 'Forget this Mortimer person. I strongly advise you to give it to Mrs Wilcox. Just as a gift you know. She takes a great interest in such things, I'm sure you won't regret it. Don't say anything about me, don't bring me into it at all. I'll tell you what, I'll buy the horse from you, I will give you . . . a pound for it. But you must give it to her yourself, just as though it is a gift from you. You keep the pound, my sister has the horse.'

He had lowered his eyes again to look at the horse. I took out my wallet, extracted a pound note, and leaning forward, carefully laid the note over the horse, covering it completely. He put the knife, which had a mother of pearl handle, down beside him, took the pound note and after a moment, began slowly to fold it. He folded it longways and then broadways. Taking this action as a token of his acceptance, I quietly withdrew.

Josh . . .

THEY DON'T KILL you with work here, I will say that. Tea breaks going on for forty minutes, I never seen nothing like it. Ever since that time I asked for a whetstone she brings me down a tray every morning. And if it's not her bringing tea it's him dodging about telling you things. Her brother. He gives me the creeps, matter a fact.

Not that I mind the tea, a course, but these days she stays on talking. She asks me questions. I dunno what to say to her most of the time, but it don't seem to make no difference. I tell her about the stall where I used to work and I tell her about Mortimer. I tell her some of his sayings but she just smiles, very slightly like. Probably beyond her. I mean she speaks very la-di-da, there is elocution there, but I don't suppose for a minute she has thought things through like Mortimer. The thing she enjoyed most was when I told her how I have to share a bed with the bloke who does the Fairy Lights. His name is Mr Walker. She asked me if he snores like and if he rolls about in the bed, hogging the blankets, and I told her Mr Walker don't do none of them things and she laughed. Mr Walker sleeps like a log, I told her, especially when he has had a pint or two. A course, the principle is all wrong, having to share a bed when you are paying three pounds ten a week, but I got reasons of my own for not minding. Anyway she listens and she laughs quite a bit and she calls Mr Walker fairy feet because of his job like. He is an electrical engineer, fully qualified, Mr Walker is. What I don't understand is why she don't send Marion down with the tea. She makes her do everything else, just about, and it would give us a chance to see each other for a bit.

Then there is this brother of hers. He has got some of his *faculties* missing, if you ask me. He is always about the place. Going on like that about birds and snakes. Mortimer said that was a lie about the snakes, they'd never just keep to one place, they would be all over. He was having me on, Mortimer said. What is the point of it though, coming up to a bloke, claiming there's poisonous snakes in the grounds? He moves his hands about all the time, all the time he's talking. He comes out of the undergrowth at me, and starts talking about birds and hides and snakes and then he's offering me money to give the horse to his sister. Something funny about that. *Perverted.* I am buying the horse, he says, but you are to give it to her. He's very la-di-da too, a course. Do not say anything, just hand it to her, she will be so pleased. Smiling, opening and closing his hands. I was surprised Mortimer agreed to it, I would of thought he'd smell a rat. But no, he said do it. You do it, he said. You give the old lady the horse, and we will await developments. (His own words.) What kind of a horse is it? he said.

We was in the bar of the Blue Post down near the front when I told him. That same evening it was, the same day he give me the money. Friday night, pay night, very crowded, half past six we started. Mortimer was on pints, I was on halves. I'm not a great beer drinker, to tell you the truth I don't like it, I have a delicate stomach, but I always go with him—he'd only go alone if I didn't. I told him about Marion, too, that same night, not just then but a bit later on. He wasn't annoyed at all at me not telling him before. What's she like, bit of all right is she? he said, and that was all, at first. He didn't seem to mind at all, which was a bit of a surprise and to tell the truth I was a bit hurt in my feelings, he didn't show no more interest in it than that. No, you give the old dear the horse, he said. He was in a good mood, he was drinking quickly, and I had to drink fast too, to keep up like. What kind of a horse is it? he said. I didn't know, he said that you had artistic prolixities, Josiah, his own words, and I could tell from the tone of his voice that he was taking the micky. There is a lot you don't know, I said. Come on, he said, don't be like that. But still in the same tone a voice. So I just put my hand in my pocket and brought out the horse. That's it, I said. If you are interested. Sarcastic like.

He took a good long look at it and then he said, But this is very good, Josiah, very good indeed, and there wasn't a trace of a smile on his face and so it was a bit like what I'd thought it would be if I'd actually of been giving the horse to Mortimer instead of only showing him it so I said straight off, I was going to give it to you, Mortimer.

What would I do with it? he said, but he still wasn't laughing, he give me a straight look and I could tell he was pleased, underneath like. Well, I blame the beer but when he didn't laugh, when he took it serious, I mean the idea of me making him a gift, I suddenly felt, well I dunno, *grateful*. And not worried any more. There was no need to say any more on the subject. I would give the horse to Mrs Wilcox or to Old Nick, it didn't matter, because Mortimer had taken it serious. This feeling come over me in a rush and my eyes started smarting. They do that. So I got up before he could see and went over to the bar and ordered another pint for him another half for me. I knew I didn't ought to be drinking any more, I felt swimmy like, but there it was.

He had not forgot about Marion a course. I might of known he would come back to her, sooner or later. You are a sly one, Josiah, he says, half way through that pint I got him, keeping her up your trouser leg all this time. What is she like then? Well, I said, then I stopped. I didn't know how to describe her to Mortimer. What I was worried about was not getting it over in the right way, not giving the right impression like. Mortimer always sees down into things farther than what I do even if it is me that is telling it, and I was scared he might see down into this and come up with something that would change my ideas about Marion and I would have to see it because it would be what I said myself only in other words. So it would turn out to be my real opinion. He has done that before, Mortimer has. I wanted him to like her but I didn't know how to bring that about. So what I told Mortimer this time was just a few facts, things she told me when she come to where I was working now and again, and we would talk. I told him Marion was an orphan, her dad died when she was a baby and her mam died when she was twelve. How she come to be in that house was that her mam was related to Mr Wilcox, they was some kind of cousins like but they never had no money. Mr Wilcox was rich because he come into a big catering business and that was how they all come to be living in this big house, but he died, Mr Wilcox did, soon after Marion came. He had a heart attack while he was pruning some roses. Anyway, they give Marion a home like. But from what I can see, I said, she earns it, the way she has to run around after Mrs Wilcox. She has read a lot, I said. She knows poems and that.

But this was getting away from the facts a course, and straightaway I seen a look come on Mortimer's face similar to when I told him about Joyce opening her blouse for me, so I went on quick. A course, I said, she's not all that good-looking, she's got buck teeth. You want to get stuck in, he said. Never mind her bloody teeth. Yes, I said. That is what I am after.

We didn't say nothing more about Marion then and I was glad, when I thought about it, that I had stuck to the facts. I didn't say nothing to him about feelings and I didn't tell him about little things she said to me like for instance when she was at school she asked the teacher if clouds had skins. If they hadn't how could they keep the rain in, she asked the teacher and she got sent out of the room. Stuff like that. She told me Mrs Wilcox dyes her hair grey. Her and her loony brother never speak to each other these days. She told me about a special way she has of having a bath when it is cold, that started when she first come to the house after her mam died. She makes herself into two people. But I never mentioned none of this to Mortimer.

No more for me, Mortimer, I said, but either he didn't hear me or he took no notice, he was at the bar ordering them, another pint for him, another half for me. Drink up, he says—I still had half the last one to finish. Drink up, Josiah, he says, but it was all I could do to get it down, and while I was starting on the next one I definitely began to feel peculiar, dizzy like and a bit on the sick side. I can't finish this beer, I said. Mortimer, I can't finish it. You got to finish it, he said. Listen, Mortimer, I said, I feel sick. Don't make me drink it, I said. You are going to finish that beer, he said, and he was getting his big-eyed look, when he looks like that there is no arguing with him. You might as well save your breath. I knew I would have to drink it in the end but I wanted to see how far I could go, so I pushed the glass a bit away from me. I won't drink it, I said. I always told you I had a weak stomach, I said. I felt scared, soon as I done it, but I wanted to see how far I could go. You drink up your beer, he said, with his teeth together like, and before I knew it I had hold of my glass again. You get that beer down your bloody throat, he said. So I drunk it, well I didn't have no choice, trying not to think what I was doing, just swallowing it down, and I felt all right for a bit. That's right, Mortimer says. That's the ticket, Josiah.

Then they called for Last Orders and Mortimer started talking in a way he sometimes has, half to me, half to himself, but in quite a loud voice. Closing time, he said. Stern daughter of the voice of God. Think of it, Josiah, he said. Use your visualising faculties, picture it on a national scale, all the pubs all over the country turning them out into the night. A million of them turned out the same time, all with a sodding skinful. If the sheer scale and concept is too much for you, think of it in concrete terms. Think of all the walls. Walls? I said. I was beginning to feel bad again. Think of it, he says. All the walls they are pissing up against, spewing up against, wanking up against, screwing the tarts up against, think of all the slimy walls, Josiah. The mind boggles. Think of all the things they are getting up to now in the back alleys and the bus shelters

and the recreation grounds, all the blood, all the vomit, all the
sperm, lakes of it, oceans of it—

I feel sick, I said. I am going to be sick, Mortimer. I got up
and got through the bar somehow, how I don't know, I could
hardly see, round to the Gents outside in the yard and I only
just got in when the first lot come shooting out of me and I
could feel Mortimer's arm round me very tight, holding me
together like, while I retched waiting for the next lot, a roaring
in my ears, stink of disinfectant, Mortimer's arm round me and
Mortimer's voice close to my ear saying, Marion wouldn't
do this for you, would she, your Marion wouldn't do this.

Simon ...

As soon as I saw Miriam coming up the drive, in lime-green, dangling a barbaric bracelet, I knew she had come for a *tête-à-tête* with my sister and I resolved to listen in. I cannot afford to neglect such opportunities. I felt it proper, however, to smarten myself up a bit before eavesdropping, wash my hands and face and comb my hair; and this, while giving Audrey and Miriam time to settle themselves on the terrace, caused me to miss their opening remarks.

Now there is a pause, presumably while they stir and sip. I hear the rattle of a cup in a saucer. In the silence of the sitting-room I picture the sunlit grounds with the secret, the slender thread of my tunnel waiting there for me. I maintain a rigid expectant posture, looking steadily at the open french window. If someone were to enter, Marion let us say, I could pretend to be looking for something, or I could pretend to be fastening my shoe laces. . . .

'Such lovely warm weather,' I hear Miriam say, and I know the expression which will be accompanying these words, the eyelids drooping, the thin lips conveying a spiteful relish.

'To give you an instance of what I mean,' Audrey says. 'Take what happened a week ago. Sometimes one feels . . . lonely.' This pause before the adjective is a familiar rhetorical device of Audrey's and again I know without needing to see it, the gallant little smile, the accompanying gesture, quite invariable, she raises her right hand and places her middle finger on the centre of the forehead, smoothing it to the right as far as the temple, as though tracing the track of a pain or soothing one away. 'One is, after all, a woman.'

'I think you manage marvellously, my dear.'

'There are situations that are difficult to deal with, for a woman alone. My brother, of course, is not a great help to me.'

'By the way, Anne wants Mr Thebus to know that she bears him no ill-will, none at all. I have seen her several times since. She is still far from well, of course, but she does not hold him responsible.'

'I do not think the responsibility is hers to allot. It was by the merest chance that the . . . object was discovered in her portion. No, it was aimed at me, quite clearly. I shall not forgive Simon whatever happens. I have told him to look for a place elsewhere.'

'Well I'm sure you're quite right dear, but Anne says now that Mr Thebus was simply the agency of an impersonal force. She has come round to the belief, she told me, that the teeth in the mousse was a symbolical revelation specially intended for her. Mr Thebus, on this view, was merely a vehicle. . . . Of course it was a shock to her, the whole system, well what a thing to find, but she told me herself it may all have been for the best, it is the sort of sudden shock, she said, that the Bhodisvattas aimed at, it *may* have put her on the track of higher things.'

'She is at liberty to take whatever view she pleases. Personally I think she's overdoing it, but that is neither here nor there. I shall continue to regard it as a disgusting practical joke of Simon's, aimed deliberately at ruining the occasion. As I say, I have told him to make other arrangements.'

'Well dear, not before time, I've told you over and over again, and as for Anne, between you and me, what I felt like saying was I hope it has put you on the track of not taking such large helpings of mousse, she is *enormous* and Dovecot seems to get thinner, they are quite grotesque together on stage, I don't know what this professional producer is going to make of them. . . .'

'Oh, they are going on with that, are they?'

'Well you know what Major Donaldson is when he gets an

idea. They have already advertised. I was against it from the start but I was overruled.'

'We must hope for the best. I hope Anne will be quite recovered in time for the garden party, I am counting on her for some help.'

'This garden party is a splendid idea of yours, Audrey. I know I am speaking for the whole committee when I say how much we appreciate your efforts . . . I believe you are going to read for the part of Mrs Alving next Tuesday evening?'

'Yes, I thought I would have a try, you know . . .'

'Well between you and me I think there is a very good chance of your being given the part, this is strictly confidential, of course, anything can happen, but I think there is a very good chance.'

'It is a part I have always wanted to play.'

'Yes, well, we must wait and see. How is your new gardener turning out?'

'He's not like a gardener at all really. He is very young, for one thing. I mean, I think of gardeners as middle-aged men with bands round their trouser-legs you know, but he comes to work in tight jeans.'

Laughter. Miriam's throaty and artificial, Audrey's a series of very rapid staccato sounds expressing not amusement at all but a quality of excitement.

'I know just what you mean, dear.'

'He is only twenty you know, that is all I could think of to ask him when he came for the job. That is what I meant by being a woman alone, a man would have known what to ask. Simon should do all that of course, he should take all that off my hands. But you know what Simon is—'

'I do, dear, I do.'

'Anyway that is all I asked him, and he said twenty and I said, but that's very young and he said, I'll be older in time. He thought that was very clever.'

One does not usually discuss a gardener in these terms, Audrey. Miriam, alerted by your volubility, says nothing.

She is hoping you will go on. I myself need no further description. I can hear the aristocratic briskness with which you put that question and he, looking too, just as you were, for a meaning in the interview, found merely a tone of voice, a smart thing to say. Did you remark his eye, the vacuity, the vulnerable boldness? A savage eye. Howard's eyes were grey, weren't they, blinking civilised eyes that acknowledged things? Ridiculous to compare of course. That little scene must have taken it out of you both in your different ways. After he had gone his gingerly way back down the drive, what was there left for you to do? It is as though some sort of rearrangement, some very subtle displacement has occurred. You walk from the drawing-room, where the interview has been conducted, and turn right, intending to go along the passage, but almost at the back stairway it occurs to you that there is no earthly reason for you to be there. So you stop at the foot of the stairs, where I can observe you from the landing. You can hear Marion in the kitchen, preparing lunch. You stand still. There is no reason for going on nor any for refraining from going. You allow your body to droop. You regard the varnished banister, the plum-coloured strips of carpet seen through the rails, oppressively familiar. Your drooping body is present to your mind, the swollen veins in your right calf, your thin arms, slack belly, dry breasts. . . . Howard is dead, his needs and the ways you met them dead. It isn't Howard you are thinking of now as you brace yourself up again, raise your head. Perhaps you have recalled some other person, someone still alive, who laid his hands on your body when you were a girl and still preserves your youth in the lecherous amber of memory, perhaps attempting to revive his failing powers with it. Or is it something the gardener said? Do you feel perhaps you will be younger in time, Audrey? Upright now, shoulders back, you pass your hands slowly over your breasts.

'He had been working up till then, by his own account, as an attendant at a rifle-range in that big fun fair down on the west shore, yes I know, not much connexion with gardening. . . .'

With the utmost circumspection I make my way out of the room, along the passage, up the stairs. The door of Audrey's room is not locked. It is cool and as it were . . . chaste, in here. Audrey strikes many persons, I know for a fact, as a rather affectedly gracious woman, too stately for most occasions. She always seems to be *dispensing* something or other to people, and while some of this may be due to shyness, I am sure myself that it is mainly because of that compulsive anticipatory quality that I believe I have mentioned before; she has adopted too soon the dignity and consequence of age. Anyone knowing only this public aspect of my sister would be astonished to find in this room evidences of another habit of mind entirely, an attachment to the past, the possessions of childhood, a sentimental sort of hoarding. A miniature tea set given to her by an uncle on her sixth birthday: small porcelain figures of domestic animals, pink pigs, a spotted dog; a row of dolls in national costume. There are drawers in this room containing little shoes she once tottered on, early suits of pyjamas, her first school uniform. And everywhere photographs of schooldays, blurred pigtailed friends, dim hockey groups, blind smiles on the promenades of remote school excursions. . . . There are no photographs of adults in the room at all, not even one of Howard. Clinging to the props of childhood, grasping prematurely for the exemptions of age, Audrey seems to have no middle period. . . .

The room was cool, hushed, neutral-smelling. My eyes turned immediately to the little table beside the pink-quilted single bed: nothing there but aspirin and Rumer Godden. The dressing table beyond presented the usual features, cut-glass bottles, brushes backed with mother-of-pearl, a light dusting of face powder. Disappointed here, I began to go through the drawers of the tallboy against the wall and in the third one I found it, lying on its side, appearing to be sniffing or nibbling at a pale-blue undergarment of my sister's. I did not realise how much importance I had been attaching to this horse until I actually saw it there, and then I experienced a sense of triumph almost suffocating in its intensity. When I was able to look closely at the horse I saw that it was now slightly discoloured along the back and part of the rump, the light-coloured wood was streaked darker. I was sure it had not been thus before. It was a stain of some kind, like paint or ink but irregular in outline as though not applied deliberately.

I held the horse in my hands for some moments, looking closely at it. It really was a remarkably fine horse. There was a passionate quality, a sort of fierce nobility in the raised head, the flared nostrils; and a suggestion of fabulous fleetness in the whole body. I ran my finger down the arch of the neck, very slowly, then I replaced it in the drawer, taking care, of course, to leave it in precisely the same position.

It was while I was actually closing the drawer, or possibly immediately after closing it that I happened to glance through the window. My sister's room looks out over the west side of the grounds, where the proposed patio is, and so I was able to see Marion and the gardener standing quite close together, talking directly into each other's faces. Marion raised her head slightly in a laughing manner and the gardener made a shrugging motion. Marion would know, of course, that Audrey was still on the terrace at the front of the house, so she felt safe here. Her hair seemed much less frizzy than usual. The gardener half turned, allowing me to see that the thumb of his left hand was heavily bandaged.

Josh ...

ART BOOKS, WHERE'D she get them all? Pictures a horses, pictures a bulls, pictures a women with nothing on, that last one art of Mesopoto something, great fat 'uns with about five hundred tits. Fertility goddess, she says. Her own words. Turning the big pages with her white fingers. Looking at me sideways, watching my face all the time. Fertility goddess, she says. Studded all over with tits, like pineapples. She did not ought to be showing me pictures like that. Symbol of fertility she says. Oh yes. I don't say nothing but personally I think it is disgusting. She'll go from that to pictures of little pot pigs, birds, anything. All in the same tone a voice. What I mean is, it don't matter to her whether it is pot pigs or bare tits. She turns the pages over fast, I never get much time to look at what is written underneath. Most of the words are too long, anyway. Oh yes. Very interesting. Look at that arm, she says. The articulation, Josiah. Have you ever attempted the human figure? The naked human form, she says, is a marvellous structure. (I am giving her own words now.) Don't you think so? she says. Depends, I says, on whose naked form it is. No, no, she says, smiling like, quite divorced I mean from sex. She keeps crossing and uncrossing her legs. She don't bother too much where her skirt is. In the abstract I mean, she says, crossing them the other way. Most of the time I dunno what she is on about. I can see right along her left leg nearly up to the top of her stocking. I would not put my hand in there any more than in a mouse trap. I can see a varicose vein right through the stocking, just under the back of her knee. The human form divine, she says, smiling round at me. She has got clean white teeth and she doesn't smell of herself but always of the clothes she's got on, just a kind of faintly scented cloth smell so I get the feeling she don't take her clothes off at night, just hangs herself up in the wardrobe, like.

Where'd she get all them books from that's what I'd like to know. Maybe she had them in the house before, stacked away somewhere. Maybe she keeps nipping out to buy one. (She don't go out so often though.) I seen the inside cover on some of them, five guineas, seven guineas, that's a lot of money for a book. She has got loads of money a course, with that big house. (But Marion says they only use four of the rooms, the others have got sheets over the furniture and nobody goes in them.) Anyrate, she has enough for books. I can't get away from it, wherever I am in the grounds, its Jo—osh, yoo-hoo, and another art book. I am not a great reader, I said to her—I told her that straight off. Not a great one for reading, Mrs Wilcox. Oh, she said, but this will help you. You must know what has been achieved in your field.

It is ever since I give her the horse. She changed after that. I could see she was struck with it at the time. The look she give me. Then the way she spoke, all sharp like to cover up that she was pleased with it. I can always sense them kind of things. It was a funny time to hand it over, just after she'd finished doing up my cut. Blood all over the place, on the floor, in the sink, all down my trousers.

Maybe I got careless, coming near the end of it like, maybe I lost interest a bit because I was not going to give it to Mortimer, I dunno, I never cut myself before, never, you won't find a scar anywhere on me, never broke no bones neither. I watched myself doing it, that was the funny thing. The knife slipped off the back and down like it was slow motion but my thumb still pressing hard on it right across the fleshy bit at the bottom of the left thumb. I didn't feel nothing and that is how I knew it was a bad cut. It was only after I stood up that the blood really started coming but it still didn't hurt. I didn't look at it because I do not like the sight of blood. I do not like thinking about it neither, even in your veins I mean, I just don't like to dwell on it. First thing I done was put the horse in my pocket. Then I started off towards the house. I was holding the cut hand palm up in the other. I got to the kitchen but there was nobody there. I thought Marion would of been there but she wasn't. It was only when I was actually in the kitchen that I looked down at my hand and I got a nasty shock because the way I was holding it sort of cupped my hand was full of blood like a bowl. Some was getting through my fingers and falling on the front of my trousers or on to my shoes. Then I got this kind of ringing in my ears and I couldn't think what to do, I didn't want to move because I didn't want to lose my blood out of my hands on to the floor, well I lost my presence of mind as you might say and I just stood there. Till she come. I was standing there with my head ringing, looking down into my handful of blood, trying to keep it from spilling, when she come in from the passage and she took it in straightaway, she's quick on the uptake, I'll say that. What are you standing there for, she said. Get it under the tap. But I was in a bit of a state by this time, I could hear what she said clear enough but I didn't want to move like. Next thing she had her hand under my elbow and she pushed me over to the sink, quite strong she is, stronger than what you'd think, and my handful of blood was splashed all over the place. She made me keep it there a long time. After that she put some stuff on it, bandaged it up. You ought to have a stitch or two in that, she said. You ought to see a doctor.

I don't need no doctor, I said to her. I got my right hand round into my left pocket somehow and I got the horse out and I handed it to her. She looked at it for a bit then she said, Where did you find this? I did not find it, I said. I done it myself. That is how I come to cut myself, I said. She still looked as if she did not believe me. I was just finishing it off like, I said. Are you telling me you carved this horse yourself? she said. She had another look at it, a good long look this time.

holding it up about six inches from her eyes then slowly moving it away, looking at it all the time, narrowing her eyes like. Well, I thought to myself, you can look at a thing without going through all that paraphernalia, but I did not say nothing a course. It is very, very good, she said, looking at me in a sort of solemn way. She started handing it back, but I said, No, it's for you. She got a surprise then and the bossy look come back on her face as if I had said something out of turn. What do you mean? she said. Maybe it was because of me losing all that blood, I dunno, but I suddenly felt like going off and sitting down on my own for a bit. It is for you, I said, and I started moving towards the door. Wait a minute, she said. She looked at me, then down at the horse then back at me again. She didn't look bossy any more. Are you sure? she said. Do you really want me to have it? Yes, I said, it's for you. But it must have taken you a long time, she said. Yes, I said, a fair old time, but I only worked on it when I had a bit of time to spare like—. Quite soon after you started here, she said. You must have begun it quite soon after starting here. . . . That's right, I said. And you had it in mind from the start to give it to me? That's right, I said, it is for you. It is quite beautiful, she said. It shows great talent. Have you had any teaching? No, I said, I never had no teaching. Good, she said, and she suddenly started smiling, she was holding the horse tight in her hand. Self-taught, she said. Like Blake, she said, and since then it's been art books.

I spend more time in the house than out of it these days, well it's all right a course, but I dunno what I am getting paid for, the only time I can get a word with Marion is in the afternoon when the old girl is having her nap and just lately I can't even get away at five o'clock, take last night for example. She was waiting for me on the terrace when I come round from putting the shears and the rake away in the shed at the back. There's something here that I think will interest you, she says, and she shows me the back of another art book. German wood-carvings of the Middle Ages, she says. You have a lot in common with these peasant artists and craftsmen, working obscurely but in a great tradition, she says. But first have a sandwich, I got Marion to make up some ham sandwiches. Oh yes, I said. I could of objected of course. It was five past five. Mortimer says I should of objected. But when I seen her sitting there with the art book like, and a pile of sandwiches all ready on a plate, I didn't feel like saying nothing. What I mean is, she had been making preparations for it and she had this sort of cheerful bossy look that meant she was enjoying herself. You can't just say, Sorry, it's gone five, and go off.

So I started on the sandwiches and I told her something about the stall where I was before I come here, how they used to work it with the elastic bands, whip them off to get a crowd up. How do you mean? she says. I don't quite follow you. Well, I said, they had these rubber bands see, that they could fix on from behind, there was blokes behind developing the photos, and if they put the bands on, never mind how many times you hit the bull, nothing happens, but if they wanted to get a crowd up they could whip the bands off and the lights would be flashing all over the place. . . . I see, she says, but that is cheating isn't it? It is all one big fiddle, I said, from start to finish. It was Mortimer who told me about that, I said, he knows everything that is going on. Oh does he? she says. Who is this omniscient person? I beg your pardon, I said. Who is this person Mortimer, who knows so much? she says.

Well a course she'd never met him, there was no reason why she should remember, but for a minute I was surprised like. It was hard imagining somebody not knowing who Mortimer is. That is my friend, I said, that I worked with on the stall. Oh yes, she said, now I remember. He is your sort of *protector,* isn't he? I dunno about that, I said. She looked at me for a bit, then she said, You can have him here for tea one day next week if you like. Show him round and so forth. I should like to meet him. All right, I said, I'll ask him. One day after the garden party, she said. He might not be able to come, a course, I said. He might have a previous appointment like. Mortimer has a full social life, I said. I didn't want her thinking that Mortimer was just a typical stall attendant. Well, if he can manage to fit it in, she said. Shall we go inside?

We went into the room through the french window and we sat on the sofa and for the next couple of hours it was these German bed posts and screens and church pews, very good work I don't deny it, and I was beginning to get really interested like in some of it, asking her to stop a bit so I could get a good look, some of that work was really beautiful. I could tell she knew I couldn't read so well, but it didn't make no difference. What I mean is, that didn't matter to her, and there is one thing I will say for Mrs Wilcox, there was things about her I didn't care for, but she would never of tried to catch me out or show me up like.

By the time we come to the end of it the light was going. She got up to draw the curtains. You must realise your great heritage, Josiah, she said. She was wearing a fussy sort of blouse with a lot of lacy bits and a black skirt. And the grey hair shining in the light. She come back and sat beside me on the sofa. Are you working on anything at present? she said. No? That is a pity. Listen, she said, have you thought of an exhibition, of holding an exhibition? I think it might be rather a good idea. Would you care for a sherry?

I liked the sherry. I don't think I ever had none before. I liked the glasses too, with them long handles. They didn't hold much though. Some more? she said. I don't think we should be drinking it so fast actually, but this is a special occasion, isn't it? And she drunk hers down, shuddering a bit at the end like. I feel that this is the start of a fruitful collaboration, she said. She poured out some more sherry. Then she come and sat down on the sofa again. She crossed her legs one way and she crossed them the other. I have been thinking, she said. I know a lot of people. In my late husband's time, she said. There was a little nerve throbbing just under her left eye. Have some more sherry, she said. This would mean our collaborating closely. To be quite frank with you I have hesitated a long time before broaching this matter to you. Yes. You may think it

cowardly of me but.... Yes, since my husband died I have
been ... asleep as it were. I have a few well-tried friends, my
books, the peace of these grounds. But in human terms, in
emotional terms.... Are you ready for some more sherry?
It would mean a very close association, Josiah.

She was talking different now, I dunno why, sort of slow and
full of meaning like you hear them sometimes on the wireless.
I did not like it. Oh yes, I said. Since my dear husband died,
she said. She drank some more of the sherry and shuddered a
bit. I have arrived at a certain peace, she said, and to tell you
the truth I am afraid of involvements, I am content to sleep
Josiah. With my books and my ... To be aroused would be
painful, she said. I do not want to be awoken.

Yes, well, I said, and I stood up. I better be going, I said.
I did not like this way she was talking. Must you? she said.
She looked up at me and I could still see the nerve throbbing
under her eye. I was confused like with the sherry and I nearly
took the wrong door, the one leading to the back of the house.
No, this way, silly, she said. She went with me to the door.
Promise me this one thing, she said, standing at the door.
Promise me that you will respect my withdrawal from life.

I didn't know what she was on about, really. She stood there
in the light from the hall, standing bolt upright like she was on
parade, looking straight at me. It was then it come to me that
she might not be quite right in the head. Yes, I said. A course,
I said. Good night then. And I started off up the drive. At the
bend I looked back. She was still standing there at attention
like, looking after me.

I turned down the drive and all of a sudden I was in the
pitch black night. There wasn't no moon at all. I could make out
the drive easy enough after a bit, the gravel was paler and sort
of shining very faint, but both sides of me was black dark, the
bushes was all massed together. I could hear my steps on the
gravel and I could hear things in the grounds, rustlings and
suchlike, but I couldn't see nothing in there, well as a matter
a fact I never looked, I kept my eyes in front of me but I knew

there was things there in the night and after a bit I got the feeling these things was moving along level with me behind the bushes on both sides of me, keeping up with me, waiting for me to make some kind a mistake. . . . I always been afraid of the dark but I never told Mortimer that. He might make me try and get over it and I know I won't never get over it. They used to lock me up in the dark sometimes, not my dad but my auntie, and I always used to start seeing nasty faces. You can keep them off by making noises or whistling, but not in digs, you can't do it in digs, people complain, and they won't let you keep the light on all night, if they see a light under the door they are knocking in no time, do you think I am made of money Mr Smith? So you have to put something round the light, all my vests have burn marks through doing that, and that is why I do not mind these digs I got now so much really because I am sharing a bed with this bloke who does the Fairy Lights on the roundabouts, who is a qualified engineer. He is a big bloke and he don't leave me much room but I don't mind the dark when I am sharing. . . .

If I'd of known she was going to keep me there till it was dark I would of refused them ham sandwiches, no thank you Mrs Wilcox. . . . Now I got to go on at the same speed, if I stopped or went faster there is something out there could take me over. There's plenty of things got every right to be out in the dark and they know each other. . . .

I come to the last bit of the drive and I am sweating, keeping myself going at the same speed, concentrating like. Then a car went past along the road and just for a second or two its lights lit up the roadway and the front hedge and I seen somebody standing there at the side of the gate, against one of the stone pillars at the side, just a white face looking towards me, then the lights was past and all I could see was the black shape of the pillar.

I stopped in the middle of the drive and everything stopped. I could taste the sherry and my head felt cold. For about half a minute nothing happened, then a voice, 'Is that you, Josh?'

coming from the gate and my heart give one bump but I knew
straightaway it was Marion and I could tell she was frightened
by her tone of voice so I started moving again, not saying
nothing, to pay her back like for scaring me. I was meaning to
go right up to the gate like that, then I thought maybe it wasn't
Marion after all and I got scared again so I said, 'Is that you
Marion?' and she moved out into the middle of the drive and I
saw it was Marion and I went up to her.

'What you doing here then?' I said. 'It's past your bed-time.'
Trying to make a joke of it like, in case she might think I had
been scared.

'You frightened me,' she said. 'When you didn't answer. I
thought it must be you though.'

I could make out her face now, just the pale shape of it,
darker where her eyes and mouth were. I couldn't hear no
more rustlings, everything around was quiet.

'I saw her waiting for you on the terrace,' Marion said.
'Well, I knew before, when she told me to make up the sandwiches, that you would be staying over.'

'Yes,' I said. 'Matters of business.'

'I don't know about business,' she said. 'I can smell drink
on your breath.'

'People always have a drink when they are doing business,'
I said. 'Didn't you know that? People have sherry and suchlike.
You don't know the world,' I said.

'Then you didn't answer,' she said, 'and I was frightened.'

'Frightened?' I said. 'Frightened of the dark? You don't
want to be frightened of the dark. The dark can't hurt you.
Do you often come out on your own like this?'

'Lately I have been. It's the only time I get to myself these
days. That and the afternoons, when she is having her nap.
She's been terrible lately. Asking for things all the time, and
she doesn't sleep hardly at all. All through the night it's drinks
of water, cocoa, aspirins, fetch me a book. I don't know what's
the matter with her, maybe it's the Change of Life. I was reading, the Change of Life can affect you in all sorts of funny ways.

Now she has started taking her rings off and leaving them about the place and she gets up in the night to look for them. That is exactly the kind of thing that happens in the Change of Life.'

'I dunno about that,' I said. I didn't know what she was on about, change of life, I never heard of it before. Mrs Wilcox didn't seem no different now to when I first come, I hadn't seen no change. I thought that maybe I would ask Mortimer, only if it was something that everybody else knew about he would laugh. 'Doesn't sound much of a job to me,' I said.

'A girl of my age needs a bit of privacy,' she said. 'I sometimes think of leaving.'

I got a bit nearer and just very lightly put my arms round her. She didn't say nothing and she didn't move, only her shoulders seemed to settle a bit as if she was a bit more comfortable like. She felt soft and her voice sounded softer than in the day and I got this feeling that the dark was doing it, making everything about her softer. 'Where would you go?' I asked her. 'You got no folks or nothing. You got no qualifications.'

'I am seventeen now,' she said. 'My mother has been dead for nearly six years now. Once when I was just turned eight she took me on the train to see her cousin in Durham, he's a farmer in a small way. He's got this little farm and he does all the work himself, him and his wife. He used to in those days anyway. They didn't have any children. It is flat country up there, but it is pretty. I can remember it very well. It is all red roofs, not like here. He grew a lot of vegetables. He had a long shed with cows in it. There was a lot of fruit trees there, apple trees and suchlike. I can remember it now, how it all looked. He asked me if I liked animals and I said yes. I do, you know, I do like animals. I fed the chickens. His name is Lipton, my mother's cousin, he was always laughing. He asked me if I wanted to stay there, not go back home, and I didn't know what to say. I didn't want to hurt anybody's feelings you know, by saying one way or the other, so I said I didn't know, and they all laughed. We never went there again, I don't know why.

I suppose my mother couldn't afford it. That's where I'd go if I left here. There's lots to do on a farm.'

She stopped a minute then she said very slow, 'Lipton. Outside a place called Castle Eden. If I wasn't here, that is where I would be.'

She said that last bit as if she meant it specially for me. 'Don't go yet anyway,' I said.

'No,' she said. 'I won't go yet.'

Neither of us said nothing for a bit, then I kissed her. 'I like you,' I said.

'I like you too,' she said. 'You know that, don't you?'

'Couldn't we sit down somewhere for a bit?' I said.

'No,' she said. 'We'd better not. You'd better go.'

'Stay a bit longer,' I said.

'No,' she said, 'maybe Mrs Wilcox will be wanting something.'

'I am wanting something,' I said. She put her face up to mine and kissed me on the cheek. Then she turned and went down the drive towards the house. I looked after her for a bit. I couldn't see nothing but I could hear her steps getting fainter. Then I went through the gate. Now I could see where the street lamps started, but it wouldn't of made no difference if they hadn't of been there, because I didn't mind the dark now. I just suddenly didn't mind it. Walking down to the bus stop I felt different, as if I had a right to be there. In the dark. As if I belonged with them things that the scared people are scared of.

Simon ...

THE DAYS BEFORE the garden party are hot, cloudless, perfect summer days. The gardener keeps away from the shrubbery, restricting himself to peripheral tasks, and this is a source of great satisfaction to me; perhaps after all he heeded my warning about snakes. Nonetheless I do not dare to resume tunnelling. I still need an hour or so each day in my sub-terranean salon, of course; but most of my time is spent walking about the grounds observing what there is to observe.

At these times I have a strange and persistent illusion that my body is moving through silence and emptiness, or rather that my body itself imposes desolation as a condition of its passage. But when I stop short, stand still and listen, this faculty seems to leave me, to be transferred to the things growing and living around me, and I am assailed by the scents and sounds of germination, rained upon, deafened, over-whelmed, obliged to move on again, resume my blighting progress. This sensation is most intense in the middle hours of the day, when the sun is hottest.

Morning is my best time, on the whole. The early watches. There is a heavy dew and the spaces between trees look very slightly smoky. On the way to my post in the corner of the grounds my trouser bottoms get quite sodden, stuck all over with little blue seeds, the grass heads. I generally make a detour to visit the robins, since they have hatched a second brood now. Walking towards the nest I impose stillness on all but my moving body. If I place a finger on the rim of the nest and very gently press downward, simulating thus the weight of the alighting parent bird, immediately the bruise-coloured mass of flesh and feather squirms violently, divides itself, five bald heads rear up blindly, split into yellow gashes, soundless but with a concerted hunger so intense it has the effect of piercing sound, a kind of miniature trumpeting.

It would seem also to be a season of activity for snails. I see numbers of them as I crouch at the hedge waiting for the woman to appear, tiny ones the colour of milk-chocolate with beautiful speckled shells. She emerges with her brush and everything else is forgotten, but when she has gone back inside and I am experiencing the depression that always follows upon her withdrawal, I become aware of them again, clambering among the moist leaves, slender plasmic creatures possessed of great acrobatic skill. Their delicate horns shrink in at a touch. As the sun gets hot they retreat into the interior, leaving glittering crystals of slime on the leaves. The dew dries, the snails retreat, the larks begin. High up in the sky one sees them embedded. Hour upon hour, through the heat, their song is sustained, to the point of relentlessness. Beyond the bungalow the wheat is tall, the stalks and ears green-gold, stiff as cane on these windless days. . . .

Several times I am able to observe Marion and the gardener talking to each other in various parts of the grounds. This is of much too frequent occurrence to be accidental. They take care, though, only to consort together at times when Audrey would not be likely to discover it. The time they most favour is early afternoon, when Audrey is resting in her room. They stand close together and appear to have a great deal to converse about. I have not so far succeeded in getting near enough to hear what is said, but I have noted that the gardener displays a much greater volubility with Marion than he does with my sister.

As far as *gardening* is concerned, he does very little these days. He very rarely comes anywhere near the shrubbery or the central part of the grounds where my tunnel is. He clips the hedges, he has tidied up the lawn ready for the garden party and weeded all along the borders of the drive and he has done quite a bit of work on Audrey's projected *patio*. But he has made no real impression as yet on the grounds as a whole. I think he would do more if left alone; but Audrey is always distracting him with tea or these illustrated books of hers. She changes her clothes for the morning and afternoon tea-breaks, appearing in things I never knew she possessed, flowered dresses, wedge-heeled sandals, chiffon scarves. The gardener is more taciturn with her and indeed does not often look directly at her. The average tea-break now lasts at least thirty minutes and on Tuesday, instead of bringing back only the tray, Audrey brought him back as well, established him on the terrace and together they began looking through another of her books. . . .

I wonder who it was yesterday, whether there had really been a stranger in the grounds. I heard the gate quite distinctly, it is an unmistakable sound to one who knows, a sound between whirring and grating. I was standing near the pond when I heard it. I moved at once of course towards the gate, but circumspectly, using the cover afforded by the privet. The accustomed stillness spread about me as I advanced. Three frogs took headers into the pond as I went by, with the faintest of plops, the minimum of displacement. Thereafter there is silence. I come out at the front hedge and look over it, down the road. Fifty, seventy yards off I see a man's back, receding, a long back held erect, in a grey flannel jacket, surmounted by a rather thin neck. Hair on the crown cut very short. I watch him take measured soldierly steps along the road, disappear from sight round the bend. Perhaps of course just a man passing, but I had heard the gate, of that I was quite certain. In my perturbation I very nearly blundered into the gardener. He was coming down the drive, away from the gate, walking very near the edge on the same side as myself. Fortunately at the last moment I heard him and was able to conceal myself, but it was a near thing. He looked as I had never seen him look before, in some extremity of illness or exhaustion, face bloodless even to the lips, mouth hanging slackly open. . . .

The robins have hatched a second brood. The fledgelings snooze until one of the parents alights on the rim of the nest then their blind heads lift and gash yellow, the membraned eyes like raised bruises. On this occasion, however, I count only four of them. I place a finger on the rim of the nest and press gently, very gently. Almost immediately the naked heads rear up their soundless vociferation of hunger, but now there are only four. I look about at the foot of the hedge below the nest. Nothing. I extend the search for several yards around: still nothing. It would not seem then to have fallen out. But what predator would take only one? Rat, weasel, snake would leave no edible morsel. I ask myself what can have happened to this fifth one. Perhaps there were never five after all, it is difficult now to be sure.

Certain, however, that there is no one in the world of whom I can enquire.

Josh . . .

I NEVER WOULD of dreamed of it. Such a thing would never of come into my mind, we are all God's creatures great and small is what I say and besides I have a weak stomach, them kind a things make me feel sick. I wouldn't of showed him where the nest was if I'd of known what he was going to make me do, not that I think he knew himself to begin with. There wasn't no plan like, it was one of them spontaneous actions. I am giving you his own word now. That is the point of it, he says. Spontaneous actions is what we need in this world today. Too much habit about, Josiah, he says. A course I can see what he means, we are all creatures a habit, like. In this day and age. I like it when he talks to me about serious things.

He always wanted to know everything I was doing. I told him everything, but he wanted to see the grounds. He wanted to actually come and see where I was working. Well he was always interested in anything I done, Mortimer was, sometimes you might think he didn't care, but I can remember a lot of times he took a personal interest. He should never of made me do that, though, it was *cruel*. A course I see what he means about us all in this day and age being in a rut like, but if anyone had told me that on such and such a day I would of been doing a thing like that, I would not of believed them. Not even afterwards I couldn't hardly believe it. I knew I'd done it a course, I felt different, not bad, I didn't feel bad, not straight away, I felt a bit out of breath as if I'd been running. And there was this other thing that happened to me, at the same time. It was only afterwards I felt sick. You have to violate your moral framework, he says. His own words. Standing there beside the hedge with the thing sitting on the palm of his hand, bluish fluff all over it, not frightened, stretching its skinny neck, trying to see. . . .

It keeps coming into my mind. I try not to think about it, but it keeps coming in. The best thing, the thing that keeps it out best, is what Marion told me about the way she makes herself into two people when she is having a bath. I haven't told this to Mortimer yet. I only told the facts to Mortimer, up to now only the facts about Marion, not any stories like. What she does, when she has a bath, is make herself into two separate persons.

Mortimer met Marion. That's why he come really. Her name kept cropping up, my fault really, well she was in my mind a lot, I couldn't help mentioning her and he asked to meet her. I wanted it too. I got her to come out in the grounds while Mrs Wilcox was having her kip. (She calls it *siesta*.) Mortimer waited near the gate. I introduced them like. My best friend. That was before we done that to the bird. Marion didn't see nothing, she'd gone back then. I wouldn't of wanted Marion to see that.

I just thought I'd show Mortimer the hide that the nutcase was going on about, his precious hide, it was only a little screen of bushes, then I showed him the nest and we had a look in at the young uns, all head and beak they was, with bumps where their eyes should be, I never touched them, never laid a finger on them, it was Mortimer that took it out. . . .

Mortimer was very polite to Marion. He knows how to behave, Mortimer does. Well, I mean, he is a man of the world. He's been a lot of places. He's never told me half the places he's been. Yes, he said and no, he said. Of course not, he said, and I quite agree with you. You're not from this part of the world are you? he said. Originally I mean. She answered him, she spoke up for herself, but she was shy you could tell, she could see that Mortimer was not an ordinary sort of person, far from it, and she wanted to make a good impression like, seeing this was my best friend. She smiled a good bit that kind of uncertain way she has, I used to think she should of had a brace for them front teeth when she was little, but I like them now, I wouldn't want to change them now. She kept looking at me a good bit and I smiled at her to show her she was doing all right like. I was feeling happy, matter a fact, seeing Mortimer and Marion talking together. But it was when they started on about film stars that Mortimer showed his ability as a conversationalist. Who is your favourite film star may I ask? he said, and it turned out David Niven was. I like *mature* men, she said. You must have had a very satisfactory relationship with your father, Mortimer said, in the same tone of voice, not making anything of it. That is just what Mortimer is like, you can't help admiring him, he isn't content just to go along on the surface, he goes straight to the root like. I don't know I'm sure, she said, he died when I was five. And she smiled like, as much as to say, not much of a relationship *there*. The first five years of life, he said, is the receptible period. His own words. I like Cary Grant too, she said. She's not really what you might call happy on the intellectual plane, a course. Well there aren't many that could keep up with Mortimer. I think she was impressed though.

I *think* she was. She never wants to talk about Mortimer, mind. If I start talking about him, she says, no, talk about *you*. I dunno what he thinks about her neither. Now that he has met her, I haven't had a chance to ask him since then. Since we done that. . . .

He stood there with the thing on his palm, talking. It kept on stretching its neck as if it was trying to see. I dunno if it could see, I don't think it could. Its eyes was open like but there was a sort of skin over them. You could see the eyes underneath, but I don't think it could of seen through, besides it didn't look at nothing, it didn't know nothing until the thorn was going in. It wasn't me that got the thorn, I would never of dreamed of it, it's not in my nature, besides I have a

weak stomach. He never meant to, I'm sure he never, not when
he got it out of the nest. He just wanted to have a look. It was
when it shit on his hand that his face changed. It was just
like it done it on purpose, biding its time then letting out a
squelchy one in the middle a Mortimer's palm, well I laughed
at first and he smiled too, but his face got a certain look I
knew because I seen it before. He didn't wipe it off neither,
that was another funny thing, he just left it there.

He looked down at it for a bit, kind of smiling. Moral frameworks, he said. I am giving his own words now. He looked at
me. I don't follow you exactly, I said. Define your terms, I said.
Do you consider yourself a good person? he says. I was just
going to say, yes a course, but that was bit flat, a bit disappointing like to Mortimer who had started this conversation, then
I remembered what Mr Harding, he works at the Pleasure
Park, was always saying about Original Sin. (His life was
changed by reading a bit of the Bible once when he was inside.)
A course, I said, there's Original Sin, we all got a touch a that.

I felt proud of this remark at the time, I didn't know a course
what it was all leading up to. I didn't have no inkling.

No, it's all habit, Mortimer said. What you have to do, he
said, is give yourself a shaking up. Every now and then you
have to perform an outrage on your moral frameworks, or it
will all only be habit. Outrage, Josiah, he said and he was
looking at me now very fixed like, not smiling any more. I
dunno what you're on about, I said, I was too scared now to
try to understand what it was about, because Mortimer's face
had gone so serious and sort of determined. No, he said, listen
Josiah. *Listen.* You don't know what I'm on about because you
never think for yourself. Your moral frameworks are blunted.
From time to time, he said, Josiah, and this is one of the times,
this . . . creature gives us our opportunity, from time to time
we have to do things that may well go against the grain but we
have to do them for the sake of our moral frameworks. . . .

I didn't like him saying that about me not thinking, so I
nodded and said a course, a course . . . . I'm glad you agree, he

said and went over to the hedge and when he come back he was holding this thorn, must of been an inch long, curved like, with a thick base, a briar thorn. Well, I looked at it and I looked at him and it still never come into my mind what he was intending, that is how I know such things is not in my nature, because I never had no inkling of it. . . .

You're an artist, Josiah, he said, so you have got a good eye. That's a pun, he said, that's a pun, by the way. I want you, he said, to push this thorn through its eye. Right into its rudimental brain, he said. I am giving his own words now.

I knew he meant it, from the way he was looking at me, not only that but all of a sudden I saw that everything we had been talking about could only mean something if it led up to this. It was something that was necessary like, and it was because of this I had been afraid ever since Mortimer's face had changed. Afraid, but not only that, sort of expecting something as well, excited really.

You must be joking, Mortimer, I said. You don't mean it do you, Mortimer? I knew he did though, and I felt my lips beginning to tremble a bit like they always do when I get worked up like or when I feel I got no protection, nowhere to turn. Now he began to look at me as if he really had made a joke and wasn't sure if I understood or not and that was like a lot of other times in my life when people told me things and waited to hear what I said with just that look Mortimer had now, and whatever I said they laughed. I got to recognise that particular expression and what I done was laugh first, without saying nothing. I'm what you call the intuitive type but you can't tell people that. So I tried it now, I laughed a bit, but Mortimer didn't laugh. He just held out the thorn on the palm of his hand. On his other palm the thing was shivering as if it was cold and its head had stopped craning and settled back on its breast like. You could see it was missing the warm nest. Mortimer's face did not look as if he was expecting anything now, he looked as if everything was decided. Please, Mortimer, I said. (He never changes his mind a course, once he says a thing.) Take the thorn, he said. Take it, Josiah. But not angry, he wasn't angry, he spoke to me very quiet and . . . affectionate—as if he was giving me some kind of help and that is how it seemed to me at that moment, as if I had something very hard to do and he was giving me a bit of help. Go on, he said. You want to really. Please, I said, please don't make me, I said, and I took the thorn, I never remembered taking it after, but I had it with my thumb against the flat base and I was still asking him to let me off but I dunno what I said because while I was talking I was doing it, near enough somehow to the thing to see the thorn going in, all the way in like it was a pin cushion till my thumb was stopped against the thing's head, no blood, nothing, it was on Mortimer's palm all the time, so easy, the thorn went in so easy with my finger at the other side of the head to hold it steady and it didn't hardly move, only it made a sort of cheeping noise when the thorn first went in, and its beak half opened and stayed like that. . . .

What Marion does when she has a bath is make herself into two persons. Especially when it's chilly like, which is nearly always. There's no heating in that bathroom at all, she told me. She stays in the bath on purpose like and the water gets colder and colder but she puts off getting out until she has to and then she pretends to be someone else. She pretends she is a poor orphan with nothing in the world, that's one part of it, and the other is a rich kind lady. When she gets out of the bath she is cold and wet but the kind lady dries her with a towel and then the poor orphan begins to get cold again so the kind lady gives her clothes, one by one. First she gives her a vest and she puts that on and she feels better for a bit but then she gets cold again so the kind lady gives her a pair of knickers and so on till she had all the nice warm things and you get the pleasure of giving them like. That really makes me smile, thinking how she waits on purpose till she is really cold again before she gives herself the next thing. I told her I'd come and do it for her, I'd be the kind old lady, I'd dry her down with a towel and put her things on for her, only too pleased, I said. Yes, you'd like that wouldn't you? she said. Still, she wouldn't tell me them kind a things if she didn't want me to think about it, picture her clothes going on bit by bit, I mean it stands to reason she wants me to have a mental picture like, but there's more to it than that, it's not so sexy because it's like her, it's just exactly like her and nobody else, to make things up like that, it's her character. You only make things like that up if you've been alone a lot. I know that because of my own life. So it's not so sexy really, well it is and it isn't, it makes me like her more but I wouldn't get a hard on thinking about it.

That's what happened to me after I done that to the bird, that's the other thing that happened to me after I pushed the thorn in, I started going stiff down below like, dunno why. It didn't die all that quick. It went on sitting there on Mortimer's palm for I dunno maybe half a minute with the thorn right through its eye stuck in its brain and during that time it shit on Mortimer's hand again and I felt like I'd been running and then I felt myself getting stiff down there, only in a few seconds it got all stiff and the bird just sort of settled over on one side and that was that. Then I slowed down, everything seemed to slow down, difficult to explain really, I wasn't excited any more and after a bit I began to feel sick.

Mortimer threw the thing over the hedge and wiped his hands on the grass. He was breathing through his mouth, I could hear him. I wondered if Mortimer's had gone stiff too, when mine did. I didn't like to ask him. Besides if I'd of asked him he would of known that it happened to me. I wouldn't of wanted Mortimer to know that. I wouldn't of wanted Mortimer explaining it, giving me the benefit of his experience like, telling me why I got a hard on just in them few seconds.

Simon ...

HE FINISHED CUTTING the lawn about three o'clock on the afternoon before the garden party. Quite early next day, soon after breakfast, I watched him carrying the trestle tables round to the front of the house and settling them out on the lawn. It was another very fine day. There were to begin with some thin clouds low down in the sky on the seaward side of the town but the sun as it got hotter licked them up. By now the sky was a deep hard blue. A breeze sprang up about this time, scarcely felt at all among the trees and in the enclosed space of the terrace and lawn, but noticeable in the open, especially on the side looking towards the bungalow and the open country beyond. A warm dry breeze, full of spice. He set up the trestles round the lawn leaving the side nearest the terrace open.

After lunch Marion came out and covered the tables with white cloths. They gleamed with an almost granulated effect in the sunshine, and the breeze kept their lower edges trembling incessantly. The tables remained thus, blank, gleaming, continuously agitated, for about an hour and then my sister and Marion appeared again bearing plates of sandwiches and cakes and setting them out on the tables. From my room I watched them go backwards and forwards, Marion pale, a little round-shouldered, mouth open slightly in the effort of getting everything right, my sister quite clearly nervous, gesturing and making energetic detours. Obviously in the crisis of the organising phase.

There were bottles of beer and a big brass tea-urn which

they carried between them, and strawberries—scores of little plates of strawberries each with a dollop of cream. I could see in Audrey's face even at this distance the drawn, suffering and yet excited look these preliminaries to hospitality always effected in her. The occasion, of course, was an important one: she was attempting to consolidate her position with the Drama Group by establishing herself as number one fund-raiser. Certainly none of the other members would have been able to stage a thing like this at home.

After they had finished Audrey retired into the house no doubt to change and so forth, while Marion seated herself in the middle of the lawn and remained there, perhaps to guard against the possible depredations of birds.

I did not wait to watch the arrivals: indeed I deliberately turned my back on the window in order to avoid doing so. I spent the next hour pleasantly leafing through my scrapbooks. After a while, however, the sound of voices from outside made it difficult to concentrate. Still without going to the window I began to listen more intently, and almost immediately I became possessed by a deep feeling of uneasiness. It was that tribal twittering again. I knew in this moment that I should have to go down and join the party. Perhaps something of profound importance to me personally was at the moment being decided. Thinking of this I became even more agitated. I closed my scrap-book, put it away and went immediately downstairs and out on to the terrace.

It was still fairly early, there was only a sprinkling of people there, standing in the area bounded by the trestle tables, talking, conveying food from time to time to their mouths. I saw no one I knew. After hesitating for a moment I stationed myself in an angle formed by two tables, on the nearer of which was a plate of chocolate éclairs. I took one of the éclairs. Not far from me there was a balding man of medium build with very large ear-lobes, as though, in the formative period, with a view to elongating them, he had worn heavy earrings, as certain primitive peoples are said to do. He was wearing grey flannel trousers and a navy-blue blazer with a badge stitched in gold thread. I caught his eye at this moment, nodded and smiled at him and waved my half eaten éclair. He returned my smile but looked away immediately, seeming rather ill at ease. I took another éclair. Several more people now arrived. The lawn was filling up, the texture of the conversation growing denser. I wondered, with a sudden anxiety which the sweetness in my mouth did little to allay, what the gardener might be up to. I had the impression that numbers of people were glancing at me and glancing away again quickly. My feeling of uneasiness increased. I nodded again at the man with the ear-lobes.

'Good, are they?' he said, glancing at me and then averting his gaze.

'The king of cakes,' I said. 'Or should I say queen?' For some reason, perhaps because of my anxiety, pronouncing this last word caused me to titter a little. He kept his head austerely averted. 'It must be wonderful,' he said, after a moment, 'to have your own few acres of land. It is beautiful weather today, isn't it? Real summer weather.'

As unobtrusively as possible I possessed myself of another éclair. My sister approached us, smiling sociably at the man beside me. 'Delighted you could come,' she said. She was wearing a lilac-coloured dress with sleeves very wide at the wrist in a mandarin style and a little conical hat of the same colour. Her smile disappeared when her gaze encountered mine. She looked significantly at a point about half way down my chest. I thought that she had perhaps seen me wolfing the éclairs, but following her gaze I understood almost immediately the reason for her disapproval and perhaps for the rapid glances of which I had been aware since coming to stand here: in my haste to join the guests I had forgotten to change my attire, and I was still wearing my old tweed tunnelling suit with its reddish impregnations of clay. There was a longish pause which I attempted to fill in by looking shrewdly up at the sky; then Audrey's instincts as a hostess prevailed: 'Have you two met?' she said. 'This is Mr Spink, who does the lighting for our plays. My brother Simon. He is interested in birds.' This last in a tone of veiled disgust. 'Why Mr Spink,' she added, 'I don't believe you're eating anything.' She raised her arm in a vague gesture, gave him a rather unfocused smile, and moved away.

'Birds of the feathered sort, did our lady hostess mean?' Spink said. The topic had emboldened him. He not only met my eye now but actually winked.

'What is that badge?' I said, rather maliciously I am afraid—I hate my hobbies to be mocked. 'What university is it?'

'Royal Corps of Signals,' Spink said. He began looking with feigned interest at another part of the lawn and was obviously about to move off when Gravelin was suddenly before us, wearing a dress of large dimensions and generous stripes cut low to expose an expanse of pink neck and upper chest. Her hair was drawn back in a chignon. She enveloped us both in the mild but relentless beam of her prominent grey eyes. 'How do you do, Mr Thebus?' she said, obviously resolved to let bygones be bygones. 'You here too, Mr Spink? Are those strawberries? How delicious!' She advanced a large reddish hand free of rings and secured a plate. 'Mm,' she said, 'delicious.' She spooned up a couple, freighted with cream. Like many greedy people she found it best to be open about things. A small gob of cream adhered to the corner of her mouth, exactly the corner, and went disregarded. I watched with some fascination the way the small globule retained its essential form and density though it was constantly being interfered with by the stretching of Gravelin's mouth. How long could it preserve itself under such circumstances? Unfortunately she now saw the direction and fixity of my gaze and licked it up with nimble, though fleshy tongue.

I began to feel oppressed now by the proximity of Spink and Gravelin. Also it occurred to me at this point that I had left the gardener too long unattended. He might have taken it into his head or been instructed to start tidying up the shrubbery, he might at this very moment be poking about in the vicinity of my tunnel. . . . I began to make some tentative motions of withdrawal, but Gravelin began immediately to speak, keeping her eyes fixed on me.

'I have such a problem with this man,' she said. I thought at first she must mean Spink, but the way in which she kept us both in her sights soon disabused me of this idea. No, it must be someone else. I stood there helplessly while Gravelin observed the statutory waiting period, the reverential silence. 'He pesters me,' she said. 'He is always at my bus stop in the morning. He catches the same bus as I do. Every morning he is there. At first it was only good morning, nice day and so on, but now he is becoming familiar. He sits beside me on the bus, attempting to strike up a conversation. He is middle-aged.' Gravelin paused to lick her sticky fingers girlishly.

'Middle-aged,' Spink said. 'Ah.'

'He is becoming familiar,' Gravelin continued. 'More and more familiar. Yesterday morning he asked me if I were comfortable in my seat. That is not the sort of question you put to people on a public conveyance. I don't want to hurt his feelings but what is a girl to do?' She looked from one to the other of us, conveying the possession of doomed beauty. Another pregnant silence was developing. 'Get an earlier bus,' I said, swiftly, breaking it.

She gave me an unfriendly look. 'I don't see why I should put myself out,' she said. 'It's inconvenient.'

'Get on at another bus stop,' Spink offered. His face bore the abstracted, slightly stricken look I had seen in other victims of Gravelin's predicaments, as of a man confronted by a trivial but unexpectedly obstinate impediment to progress. 'That's what I would do in your place, get on at another bus stop.'

'Why should I change my habits?' Gravelin said. 'It's not as though it were my fault, is it?'

Suddenly I knew that I could endure no more of this. 'Evidently an impasse,' I said lightly, edging out of my corner and round Gravelin and so away.

I had intended to pass straight into the grounds and locate

the gardener, but found myself now quite close to a group of people surrounding my sister, who was speaking in a hurried, rather breathless but absolutely unfaltering voice:

'It was the *mindlessness* that amazed me, don't you know, sheer primitive mindlessness. Not the pain of the cut. The cut was rather a deep one but it wasn't that that bothered him, he simply didn't know what to do. . . .'

She is standing with her back to me but I know what expression she will be wearing, an affected humorousness only partially concealing her underlying excitement, and now for the first time I realise how obsessed Audrey is on this subject, she is no longer concerned with suitable social contexts, with *relevance*. She seems to think that the gardener, like God, can be referred to at any time, without preliminary description of the being in question. What are the people round her making of it? Their faces look immensely stolid and inexpressive. I see Miriam Daintry in a floppy red hat, Major Donaldson looking hot and rather sleepy, Dovecot's Adam's apple as still as a stone, two unknown youngish men both in grey suits.

'He simply allowed the decision to be indefinitely postponed. In that moment, he emptied his mind, you may not believe that is possible, but he is very . . . elemental. He just stood there and the blood dropped on the floor. . . .'

That was blood then, on the horse, not paint or dye. He must have given it to her at the same time. And the bandage, so conspicuous in the sunshine on the gardener's thumb. That was blood then, on the horse. She doesn't say a word about the horse, though.

'Fortunately I went down to the kitchen at the moment. He did everything I told him. I had to lead him over to it, hold his hand under it, he seemed to have no power of . . . independent motion . . . .'

There is a sort of gaiety in her tone, not at all congruous with the subject, which is after all blood and confusion, an irrepressible gaiety which renders her words intensely disturbing to me. Surely I am not alone in detecting this incongruity? Gravelin

and Spink have now joined the group. There are, in fact, only
two main groups now: that surrounding my sister and the other,
entirely female, centred on the Reverend Ede, who is to draw
the winning number, whose resonant voice I hear now saying,
'We live in an age of immense potential for good or ill. . . .'

'He was white,' Audrey says, 'under his tan. I told him he
could have a day off but he didn't want to.'

'Well, that's a wonder,' Major Donaldson says, doubtless
speaking from a deep knowledge of malingerers acquired in the
army. He speaks in normal tones; none of the others look
in any way disturbed.

'What impressed me most, as I say, what I chiefly remember,
is this extraordinary *docility*. You'll think I am exaggerating. . . .'
A humorous glance round the faces, submitting herself to their
judgment, secure, however, in really being the one involved.
Of course several will privately think that she is heightening
the occasion, gilding the whole thing so she can gleam in it too,
part of the picture, part of the artist's conception—Audrey
has always seen herself as a figure in the foreground and not
only there but outside it too, strenuously publicising the
work. . . . Nothing about the horse, though, not a word about
the horse. Even if I did not know it was there, up there in her
room, I should know there was something more, something
splendid in her mind which gives a special vividness to the way
she tells us what she is willing to impart. No, the horse clearly
is for herself alone. What she attaches to it is incommunicable.
And yet what a marvellous finishing touch it would provide, for
just such a gathering, the bloodstained horse. My wonder at
her reticence increases as I imagine how she would tell it,
the dramatic pauses, the obvious attempts to manipulate her
audience's responses, all the marks of a rotten actress. And at
the end of all this my dears, what do you think happened?
Just when I thought he had lost his wits completely, no flicker
of expression on his face at all, he handed me the little wooden
horse that he had carved for me himself and it had taken him
weeks to do. . . .

Yes, quite a temptation Audrey, but I am delighted that you don't succumb. Nothing could have expressed more clearly than this forbearance how much you value that gift.

I directed myself diagonally across the lawn intending to take the nearest way into the grounds on the side to the right of the drive, the side where my tunnel begins. This involved passing quite close to the group dominated by the Reverend Ede. By a most unfortunate chance, as I was passing, our eyes —mine and the Reverend Ede's—met, and I seemed to detect in his amiably quizzical expression an intention of addressing me or perhaps the consciousness of just having addressed me. Helplessly responding to this look, indeed quite as if impaled on it, I came to a stop, smiling and nodding my head in acknowledgement but already his face was changing, reforming as it were, and I realised too late that I was mistaken, only at this moment had he become aware of me, and he thought, of course, that I wished to attract his attention, he was regarding me expectantly. I continued to smile, trying to think of some appropriate remark that, once uttered, would enable me to move on into the freedom of the grounds, but nothing came to mind. The Reverend Ede seemed equally at a loss. He did not, however, take his eyes off me. The ladies round him had fallen silent, one or two of them glanced round. I raised my hand in a gesture of greeting and suddenly into my whirling brain came the memory of the new public lavatories opposite the church-yard gates. Some fortnight previously, in passing, I had looked in and been impressed by the immaculate white tiles, the soothing hush—an atmosphere not unlike that of the church itself. Unable to move on and equally unable to endure the silence any longer, I began to speak about these lavatories to the Reverend Ede, although I had no reason to suppose him in any way connected with them. 'I would like to congratulate you on those new lavatories,' I heard myself saying. In my nervousness I spoke with offensive familiarity. 'I don't know how far ... but I have long felt the need....' The Reverend's face had become quite expressionless now, though he continued to regard me intently. 'The ones opposite the church, I mean, there are no others as far as I know for miles, convenience in this case is no misnomer, especially for the aged who, let us be frank . . . , yes, your parishioners, in all walks of life, will feel the benefit. . . .'

The Reverend Ede at this point spoke, his lips moved, but I was confused and heard nothing. I beg your pardon? Especially in the wintry weather, emerging from your church, those lavatories. . . . I beg your pardon?

I was about to step nearer to him, but my sister approached vivaciously, spoke to him about drawing the tickets for the raffle soon, she was saving the situation again of course, his eyes slid away from me, at last; 'Entirely as you see fit dear lady,' I heard him say, as I hurriedly resumed my way out of the enclosure formed by the tables, into the grounds. I was aware that my departure had been closely observed by almost everybody.

The voices are still audible behind me, indeed very close, but the people are invisible. I move forward, away from the voices, through the trees, through patterns of sunlight and shadow, breaking without violence these patterns, sensing their immediate reforming behind me, the resumption of precise inviolate rays. With every step the sounds recede, my confusion lessens. I am aware of course that by appearing in my tunnelling suit and addressing to the Reverend Ede those unsuitable remarks I have lowered my stock still further with Audrey, but in spite of this, I am not so afraid for myself as I was before. I feel in control of events, through my secret knowledge of the existence of the horse, my sense of having engineered that whole occasion. This gift has fixed them in a relation to each other and to me. They are no longer free to range destructively. My endeavour now must be to choose a time when the feeling between them is taut, a time of tension, and then snap the thread as it were, hoping for a recoil violent enough to propel the gardener out of our lives for good, deflect at the same time my sister's displeasure from me. . . .

Gaining the shrubbery, I feel the sun hot again on my back. I entertain briefly the idea of going across to my corner to see if the bungalow woman is anywhere about but my overwhelming desire just now is to get down into my tunnel, to sit down there for a while completely motionless, and *rest*. My efforts to penetrate my sister's thoughts, or rather to impose on Audrey the thoughts she should be thinking, to forge thoughts for her, have quite tired me out. Moreover, I feel that I need very urgently the detachment that being below the earth gives me. I am tramelled up with all these persons, my sister and Marion and the gardener and the members of the Drama Group, it is as though we are all snared in repulsively adhesive strands or coils, hideously squirming together. Only down below can I be free of them for a while.

I made my way therefore, circumspectly but without excessive caution, to the point among the rhododendrons where my tunnel begins. Making sure that there was no one in the drive and no one in view in the roughly semicircular area between where I was standing and the thicker bushes on the nearer side of the pond, I ducked down quickly and crawled under the bush.

I inserted myself into the entrance shaft, replaced the trapdoor and sank to my knees preparatory to entering the tunnel. I had the torch on me—I am never without it—but preferred for these first few moments to remain thus, on my knees. When I felt sufficiently restored by the darkness, the narrow confines of the shaft, I entered the tunnel, switching on the torch at the same time.

I proceeded as rapidly as possible to the side turning and crawled down into my subterranean salon. Going across to the corner on hands and knees, I lit the paraffin lamp and squatted back on my heels waiting, while the light brought the room immediately into familiar focus, even the rosy half-light before the wick was turned up, the various things disposed about asserted almost with violence their familiarity, their quality of being objects that, however common in themselves, have a uniqueness of placing, of consideration in my mind. I turned the light up gradually, it whitened, and things assumed their placidity of existence here below, as though it had never been dark at all. The goddess or nymph, yellow-skinned and heavy-lidded, still dreamed in her nudity among the olive trees, pale tapering fingers screening the pudenda, as if no interval of time had elapsed since I saw her last.

I turned myself rather laboriously about, intending to go over to my stool and sit on it, but I became aware at this point that a certain invasion had taken place: vivid glints against the wall, the faint collisions of imprisoned wings. I saw it come to rest just below the roof, wings close together, a Red Admiral butterfly, and at practically the same moment I saw a spider's web just beyond the butterfly at the junction of wall with ceiling and the spider itself motionless at the centre. I did not know which to wonder at most, the presence of the butterfly, a creature of sunlight and the upper air, or the spider's industry in anticipation of further flyers.

The butterfly was evidently exhausted, it did not move as my hand approached it. I took the soft powdery wings between finger and thumb, aware already of damage irreparably done to their delicate texture. The legs clung for a moment to the wall with a gentle adhesiveness so that detaching the creature finally was curiously like plucking a very fragile flower. Holding it still by the wings, I turned the lamp down and blew out the flame. Then, with the aid of my trusty torch, I climbed out into the tunnel again and continued along it until it came to an end. I knew myself now to be in more or less the dead centre of the grounds, immediately below the thicker part of the shrubbery. This is where I had been working when that interloper of a gardener first appeared on the scene. Had it not been for him, I reflected, I should probably have been able to take the tunnel clear across the grounds by this time, right to the farther hedge.

I shone the torch down on to the thing in my hand. Its legs had ceased to move, they were coppery in the light, and the butterfly appeared artificial, jewelled. Its wings glowed, colour strained through the drab backs. Switching off the torch I put up my hand and raised the trap-door. Immediately sunlight rushed down on to my head and shoulders, my eyes ached, the colours of the butterfly paled. I raised my arm well above ground level and released it, giving at the same time an upward impetus with the fingers that held it. The creature dropped almost to the ground then fluttered up again higher and higher until it was lost in the sunlight. I was about to duck down again into the tunnel when my eye, which had risen above the surface of the ground to watch the butterfly's flight, caught through the ramifications of the bush nearest me, through the close mesh of the lower branches, a momentary glimpse of white, gone again immediately as my head in motion lost the particular configuration of branches which had allowed the view. Carefully and slowly, moving my eyes laterally by very slow degrees I sought again that minute and fortuitous gap. I had it again, this time there was no mistake, again I caught that glimpse of white, clothing surely, about fifty yards off as far as I could judge. Moving with great care, I raised myself up and on hands and knees emerged from the shaft. I remained still a few moments, from a primitive sense of cheating any expectations my entry into the upper world might have aroused. Then, kneeling up, I looked over the top of the same bush, through the thinning leaves. The sight that met my eyes was clear and open, so far from any attempt at concealment that for some moments my devious heart refused to credit it: not forty yards away, full in the open, the gardener and Marion were standing motionless, locked in each other's arms, engaged in a protracted kiss. With a startled particularity I noted the exact position of his dark arms across her white jersey back, exactly parallel, one across the middle of the back, the other against the waist, both his hands flat slightly splayed, one directly above the other, pressing her against him. There was a feeding intensity about his lowered head, a distraughtness in the surrender of her raised one. Beneath the white skirt her bare legs were lost, forgotten, the toes turned inward like a cloth doll's because her weight was not on them but taken in the gardener's arms, supported against his body. The kiss went on, soundless and motionless, until there was finally something of horror in its continuing. Then I saw their faces part but still regard each other closely, and as it seemed, anxiously.

Behind me, from the direction of the lawn, I heard a sudden outcry, a kind of concerted acclamatory chorus, and I realised that at that moment the Reverend Ede must have drawn the winning ticket out of the bag. And with this sound ringing in my ears I perceived that here perhaps was an opportunity for snapping that thread, causing that recoil.

As quickly as possible I covered the entrance to the shaft. Then I made my way, on hands and knees for the first dozen yards or so, back through the shrubbery, into the cover of the trees, towards the lawn. The tribal sounds gained in volume as I advanced but I experienced no faltering. I composed my features, resolved on no gestures, rehearsing mentally as I went along the respectful way in which I would draw Audrey aside, yes, if necessary, even from the side of the Reverend Ede himself, and intimate to her what her protégés were getting up to in the grounds. . . .

Josh ...

I NEVER THOUGHT Mortimer would of brought someone else with him when he come to meet me. There was no reason why he shouldn't a course, but he never said nothing about it before. They come in together. I was waiting in the cafeteria, I went there straight from work. They come in together, laughing over something. This is Lionel, Mortimer said. He is working on the stall now, he is the one that got your job. Pleased to meet you, I said. I didn't take to him at all, right from the start. He was a fattish bloke with greasy fair hair and a round face and a little wet mouth. He was older than me, about Mortimer's age. As a matter a fact he looked to me like a typical stall attendant and I didn't understand what Mortimer saw in him. He didn't say nothing back to me when I said, Pleased to meet you, he just looked at Mortimer, still with a sort of laughing look on his face. That is not how you behave when you are introduced to someone.

How's the boy? Mortimer said. Lionel went to get two teas. I'm all right, I said. There was a bit of trouble at work this afternoon. Oh yes? he said, what was that then? I'd prefer, I said, to tell you later. And I give a look towards Lionel, who was standing at the counter getting the tea. Right, Mortimer said, as if he was not particularly interested. So I didn't say nothing more, two can play at that game.

Lionel blew on his tea to cool it. That was another thing that put me off him. I mean, if your tea is too hot, you just wait, you don't blow on it. Also he neglected his person, he had hairs growing out of his nose. Look at that, look at them tits, he said all of a sudden. He was looking at one of the women serving the tea, she must of been over forty. I could do her a bit of good, he said. He talked in a funny way as if his mouth was full of spit.

Lionel and me will be having a pint or two later on, Mortimer said. At the Blue Post. Would you like to join the revels, Josiah? I couldn't understand why he was talking to me in this way, sort of not caring. As if we didn't know each other so well. He was different with me all the time Lionel was there. A course I didn't let on that I noticed. I got my self-respect. Anyway I couldn't go with them. No, I said, I can't. I'm going out tonight. That must be with Marion, Mortimer said. Going hedging and ditching, are you Josiah? He was smiling but I knew he wasn't too pleased. Lionel stopped looking at the woman and looked at me. Mortimer had guessed it, a course. I was taking Marion to the pictures.

I have been thinking about that Marion of yours, Mortimer said, and he got a certain look on his face. I tried to think of something to say to change the subject, but I couldn't, nothing come to mind. I wanted to hear his opinion of Marion but not in front of a third party as you might say, and certainly not in front of someone like Lionel.

Yes, Mortimer said, and the conclusion I have come to is that she's had a length or two slipped into her one time and another.

Lionel laughed, but I didn't look at him, I was looking at Mortimer all the time. Mortimer wasn't laughing at all. How could you of known that? I said. You only talked to her for half an hour. How could you of known?

It's easy when you know what to look for, Lionel said. He was still laughing and I knew at that moment that Mortimer had said something to him before about me and Marion. I looked at Lionel and I seen the spit in the corners of his little mouth. Seeing him sitting there laughing, and Mortimer encouraging it like, when he knew it was something just between the two of us, well it upset me, when we were on our own was a different matter, but he never done it in front of anyone else before.

Not just someone, Josiah, Mortimer said. Old Uncle Tom Cobley and all. It's the way they walk. It is their *gait*, Josiah. I have made a study of it. Particularly the way the legs go devious from the vertical, that is what you have to watch out for. Your Marion is slightly bow-legged, to use a non-scientific term, proving that she has been raising and opening them more or less steadily ever since she knew what it was for.

Do you mean you can tell just by watching them walk?

I have rarely seen a more well developed specimen than that Marion of yours, he said. Just by watching them walk? I said. Certainly, he said.

I looked at Mortimer's face and it was as if I had never seen it before, just for them few seconds he was like someone I didn't know and I got this feeling that he didn't care what Marion was really like. Always before, I accepted everything Mortimer said, so now I tried to think what Marion walked like, but I got confused because now he had said them things about her I couldn't keep clear in my mind what I thought about her before. Mortimer has this way with him, once he has said something on a subject, it isn't the same, you can't feel the same exactly as you felt before. But Mortimer gave himself away by what he said next. Maybe if he hadn't of said nothing more, I dunno, maybe I would not of questioned it. Or maybe if Lionel hadn't of been there. What Mortimer said was, That Marion has seen more pricks than you've had hot dinners, Josiah. It was then, it was when he said that, that I started not believing it.

You said that same thing about Joyce, I said. What are you on about? he said, and he looked at Lionel. That made it worse a course. You said that about Joyce, I said, and I understood something then, I could see Mortimer was not really interested in giving me the benefit of his advice, I needn't of bothered to give him only the facts about Marion, I needn't of been so careful, because nothing I told him about her made any difference. And I felt something else at the same time, behind this other thing, and that was Mortimer did not have the same kind of feelings I did, and it wasn't just him being a man of the world but something maybe only Mortimer felt, there was something in his ideas different from everybody else's. And I knew then that what he was saying about Marion wasn't what was in my mind before, but only in his.

You only said that, I said, because you know I like her. And I don't believe you, I said, I don't believe you can tell just by watching them walking. They could all have Plastic Surgery, if that was the case.

I do not think I would ever of spoken to Mortimer like this if he hadn't of tried to show me up in front of a typical stall attendant like Lionel. (I never looked at Lionel again the whole time he was sitting there.) I was frightened myself by this time, because Mortimer didn't say nothing, he just looked. I tried to look back at him but I couldn't. I went on talking though. You can't tell, I said, you can't, not just by watching them walk. I couldn't hardly swallow, my mouth was so dry inside because I was contradicting Mortimer like this, something I never done before. I dunno what would of happened, but just then old Mr Harding come in for his break, he works in the Amusement Arcade, giving out change, and maybe Mortimer was just as glad of it as me, because he started on at him right away. Here's Lord Nuffield, he said, putting a smile on. (Mortimer always makes out Mr Harding is rich through giving out short change.) Lend us a couple of quid, Uncle, he said.

Peace on this house, Mr Harding said, cheerful-like, but meaning it. He always says that when he comes in anywhere. Mr Harding is very religious. He went up to the counter and got his tea then he come back and sat down with us. He pulled at the strap of this big satchel he has for the change, working it round from his side till it was resting in his lap. Then he started sucking up the hot tea. He made a lot of noise doing it, well he don't know any better. He's had a very hard life, Mr Harding has. He was holding the cup in his big red hands and you could see half way up his arms, his jacket sleeves was so short, and that is another reason Mortimer makes these jokes about him being rich like, because he always wears such old clothes that I wouldn't be seen dead in myself. He don't care about clothes, a course. He is a big bony bloke and he is very strong. He stands about all day and half the night in the Amusement Arcade, digging in his satchel for coppers for people who want to have a go on the slot machines. He always looks happy.

Somebody must of put a tanner into the juke box because Eartha Kitt come on, singing *Monotonous*.

Tell us, Mr Harding, Mortimer said, what is the secret of your financial aspirations and success? Give us a tip or two.

Mr Harding looked over his cup at Mortimer for a minute. He has blue eyes and he looks at everything in the same kind of way, whether it's a cup a tea or a person or just the wall, like. The peace that passeth understanding, he said to Mortimer.

I am talking about *money*, Mortimer said. He has no time for religion a course.

Mr Harding supped up some more of his tea. Mock not, he said. He has these round blue eyes and lots of wrinkles in his face, dirt in the wrinkles, and he keeps his hair about a quarter of an inch all over.

I have known the peace that passeth understanding, Mr Harding said, since I accepted Christ as my personal saviour. Is that right? Mortimer said, in a sort of gentle way I wasn't expecting. Personal saviour, eh? he said. In them days, Mr Harding said, I used to drink. He sat up in his chair and you could see how thick his shoulders was, under his old black jacket. Four policemen, he said. It took four coppers to get me to the station. I never knew me own strength in them days. Is that right? Mortimer said, still in the same kind of voice. You got no proof, though, have you, that's your trouble. Proof? Mr Harding said. I've proved it in me own life, since I accepted that Christ died for me. That's not proof, Mortimer said. You have had no legal training, you don't know the rules of evidence. Doesn't it occur to you, doesn't it enter your cranium, that plenty of people in the antiquity era managed to live without getting drunk and knocking coppers about? Centuries before Jesus Christ was even thought of, before he was so much as a gleam in the Holy Ghost's eye, they were managing without those pleasures, Mr Harding. That was blasphemy what you just said, Mr Harding said. That was sheer blasphemy. Forgive them for they know not what they do. They lived lives, Mortimer said, of a most salutary character and without all this self-congratulation, if you'll forgive the liberty, Mr Harding. Take those classical Greeks for instance, Perikles, Brutus, all that lot. Take Socrates. What was that name? Mr Harding said. Is it pagans you are talking of? I am a living witness to my redeemer. I know that my redeemer liveth.

Mortimer got up and put his hands on the back of his chair. You think it over, he said. Just because you cut out the booze doesn't prove Jesus Christ died for you at all. Just you think about those classical Greeks.

We started to go out. Let not sin reign as king in your mortal body, Mr Harding shouted after us as we were leaving.

Like talking to a brick wall, Mortimer said when we got outside. I think I shook him a bit though. I think I gave him food for thought. Well, I heard Lionel say, I better be getting back. I didn't look at him at all. Yes, Mortimer said, that old cow will be missing you. See you later then, Lionel said. Mortimer and me stood just outside the cafeteria watching Lionel walk away through the crowd. Where's he going then? I said. He is going back to the stall, Mortimer said. He's on till nine. Oh, I said, he just happened to be having his break then, when you were coming off? That's right, Mortimer said. Oh, I said, I see. I felt a lot better now that I knew Mortimer hadn't asked him along on purpose like. I didn't think much of him, I said, but Mortimer didn't answer.

I am going to change my tactics with that old hoary Harding, he said, after a bit. Every time I see him now I'm going to insinuate a doubt. A bloke like that, he has never been argued with. He goes on telling everybody about being washed in the blood of the lamb, and nobody says anything. What's the point? I said. I mean, he's happy enough, he don't do no harm. Mortimer looked at me for a minute, pressing his lips together. You are in a contradictious mood this afternoon, aren't you Josiah, he said. He's ignorant, he said, and all of a sudden he looked angry again. Ignorant old bastard, he said, going round spreading all that shit. There's no Christ or angels waiting to save us. If this country was run on rationable principles he would be prosecuted for spreading the sentimentalist point of view, it's worse than the pox because there are no injections for it. I hate all that shit. I am a realist. Oh, I said. Realist. And he is a sentimentalist, Mortimer said, and he is a soft-headed old bastard into the bargain, but I'll fix him.

I said them words to myself a couple of times, trying to get them fixed in my mind. I could see it was better to be a realist a course.

What happened at work then, what was that bit of trouble you mentioned? Mortimer said. So I told him how I was with Marion and we thought we was safe right at the other end of the grounds with everyone on the lawn having their tea and waiting for the raffle so we didn't bother to hide like, not thinking it worth the trouble and not having much time in any case, she only got away for a few minutes, then I happened to look over Marion's shoulder and there's Mrs Wilcox standing looking at us in this pointed hat that was not suitable for a woman her age as I thought when I first saw it, God knows how long she had been standing there, she just stood and looked and I could hear her breathing, well more like gasping, and Marion must of sensed something because she stood away from me and we both looked back at Mrs Wilcox. I dunno what she looked like with this dead white face and her lipstick and that hat. Get back to the house, she said to Marion in a voice I never heard her use before, the words come out like spitting and Marion was off like a rabbit, without a word. Mrs Wilcox looked at me for a bit longer and I was expecting her to say you're sacked but she said nothing just turned away and went back through the bushes. She didn't seem to look where she was going because she walked right into one bush and then got round it and disappeared. Well it was quarter to five like, so I just packed up and got on the bus and come down to the Pleasure Park and waited in the cafeteria.

I expect I'll get my notice tomorrow, I said. No, Mortimer said, I don't think so. I know the sort she is, I have got her weighed up. I was expecting him to say a good bit more but he didn't, and that was disappointing because I wanted to hear his views, he might of given me a lead. I'll be getting back to my digs, he said. By the way, the old girl said I could come to tea, didn't she? Ask her if I can come next Sunday. Just ask her. All right, I said, I'll ask her. Will you be able to get off the stall? I'll fix that, he said. Are you sure you won't be coming tonight? Yes, I said. I can't. I got to meet Marion. Cheerio then, he said, and he walked away. I watched him walking away through the crowd. He was taller than most and he kept his head up. There was no one to compare with him like, in all that crowd, and watching him walk away I felt all alone and I thought, What would I do if Mortimer was going for good like, if I was never going to see him again.

I might as well of gone with them as it turned out, because Marion didn't come. I waited for her three-quarters of an hour, till the big picture was half over, but she never come. I could still of gone to the Blue Post, it was only half past nine, but I didn't feel like it, not with Lionel there. I was afraid Mortimer would be different with me again, if Lionel was there. He might make me drink up, like last time. I had a cup a tea and a sandwich, then I went back to my digs. When I got there I found that the qualified engineer that does the Fairy Lights, by name Mr Walker, had gone, and I was sharing with a new bloke, a little bloke from Derbyshire that he told me he was a miner, he had had an accident down the mine and he come for a bit a sea air, a rest cure as you might say.

I thought at first it was a bit a luck because Mr Walker is a very fat man and he used to take up all the bed, so when I saw this new bloke I thought to myself, this is only a little 'un, like me, he won't take up so much room, but it turned out worse than ever because he had a bad hip as a result of his accident and every time he laid on it he jumped and groaned like, and it woke me up. Well, this must of happened a dozen times through the night.

Next day was Sunday. I wasn't feeling so bright. About one o'clock I went round to the café where Mortimer usually has his lunch but he never come. I thought maybe he was with Lionel somewhere, having his lunch in a different place that Lionel knew about. All afternoon I was walking, on the front mostly. I had three cups a tea at different places. I never went near the stall a course. I was wondering why Marion never come to meet me. But mostly I was thinking about Mortimer and Lionel together on the stall, getting on together. I thought maybe Lionel isn't just a typical stall attendant after all, maybe Mortimer is taking up with him. It kept coming into my mind, and I wished I hadn't of argued with Mortimer and contradicted him. Nine o'clock I waited near the entrance to the Ghost Train, just round the corner from it, where the Guess Your Weight man stands. Mortimer has to come past here on his way home. I was going to say, I'll have a drink with you tonight if you like, but when he come past he had Lionel with him. They was talking together and Lionel was laughing. I did not let on I was there. I went to bed early but I never got much sleep, what with thinking about Mortimer and Lionel, and then this bloke heaving and groaning all night long.

I never seen Marion till the Monday afternoon. Mrs Wilcox

never come near me, she never brought no tea and I did not
like to go near the house so I did not get my tea-break. Then
about three o'clock Marion come down to where I was working
near the front hedge. She was wearing the dress she nearly
always wears about the house, pale brown with three-quarter
length sleeves and a belt. I was going up to her like, but she
said no, don't, I don't feel safe any more, since Saturday. I'm
sorry I didn't come on Saturday night, she said. I waited,
I said. I waited an hour. Oh I *am* sorry, she said. I didn't
think you would wait so long. But she was pleased, I could
tell. More like an hour and a quarter, I said. What happened,
then?

Well, it was Mrs Wilcox, she said. She never spoke to me
or looked at me till after supper. I did the washing up and
tidied up in the kitchen as I always do. Then I went upstairs
and started getting ready. When I was in the middle of it, the
bell rang. I went down to the sitting-room and she was was in an
armchair with just one table lamp on and she said, Get me two
aspirins will you, I have a terrible headache. So I went and got
them and a glass of water and I put them on the table beside her.
She had her eyes closed all this time. I was going away again
when she said, Please don't go. She must have heard me. Stay
and talk to me, she said. I didn't say anything straightaway and
she opened her eyes and looked at me, well she must have
noticed that I had changed my dress because she said, Are you
going out? I said, Yes, it is Saturday night. Oh yes, she said.
I had forgotten that. She was as white as a sheet. Marion, she
said, since your mother died I have felt as it were, responsible
for you. I stand to you instead of a parent, she said and I don't
want you to think I haven't got your interests at heart, you are
so young and inexperienced and there are people who would
take advantage of that. Life is full of pitfalls she said, for a
young girl like you. Are you going anywhere special? she said.
Only to the pictures, I said. She closed her eyes again. I asked
her if there was anything else and she said no, so I went back
upstairs. Then half an hour later, I was just about ready to go,

she rang again. She was still sitting there, the aspirins were still
there beside her. Marion, she said, I want you to stay at home
with me tonight. I am feeling unwell, she said, and I need
you here. She said this in a sharpish sort of way and I was
going to say well, it *is* Saturday, but when I looked at her face
I saw she had been crying. Just sitting there crying to herself.
Well I wanted to see you, I really did, but I had no choice
really. I had to stay with her.

Yes, I said, a course, that's all right. What was the matter
with her, then? Oh, she said, she cheered up after that, she
didn't say much to me at all. I sat there listening to the wireless
and she played patience.

She wanted you to stay in so she could play patience? It don't
make no sense to me, I said. Anyway, never mind, there is
always another time. I don't want to meet you in the grounds
any longer, not after what has happened, she said. You see that
don't you. But I can't go all day, I said, without seeing you.
Do you really mean that? she said. A course I do, I said.
How can I go a whole day without seeing you? I wish I knew
if you meant it, she said. Honest, I said. Honest I mean it.
You don't look so well yourself, she said. Your eyes are a bit
bloodshot. Have you been drinking? No, I said, it's not drinking, I haven't been getting my sleep. I told her about the new
bloke I was sharing with. I made it seem funny like, imitating
how he heaves and groans, and she laughed quite a bit. It is
funny, I can make people laugh sometimes, but I can never
make Mortimer laugh. He don't laugh often a course. You will
have to change your sleeping partner, she said. Yes, I said, I'd
like to do that, and I gave her a look. Who would you like to
have instead? she said, pretending not to know what I meant.
You know who I'd like to have, I said. No, I don't, she said.
If you don't you ought to by now, I said. Would you sleep
any better? she said, and I tried to get my arms round her,
but she stepped back. I'd better be going, she said. It's time I
was getting the tea. But where can I see you? I asked her, if
you don't want to come into the grounds. She looked at me a

minute, still laughing like, from what we'd been saying, then while she looked at me her face went serious and I could see in them big brown eyes of hers that she really liked me. I know a place, she said.

Simon ...

WHOSE THE WINNING number was I never sought to enquire. I did not return to the garden party after betraying Marion and the gardener to Audrey. I was too overwrought. I spent the remainder of the afternoon and the evening in my room. So I do not know how she managed the situation, how she conducted herself among the guests afterwards. That my plan had failed, however, that she had not dismissed the gardener, became clear to me during the following week as I watched him go about his business quite as if nothing had happened. She appeared to avoid him for a day or two, but my hopes were finally dashed on Wednesday morning when I saw them sitting together on the terrace looking at a book, one of those books which are now lying everywhere about the house, large and lavishly illustrated, dealing with Roman coins or Etruscan figurines or Hellenistic bronzes. The gardener's education had obviously been recommenced. On Thursday evening he stayed on after work and was given drinks in the drawing-room.

Audrey at this time took to dressing more youthfully, in square-necked, short-sleeved blouses and high-heeled shoes. She wore her hair too in a softer way now, not drawn back but framing her face. She did not, however, regain the look of happiness that she had had before the garden party. Her mouth seemed to have thinned, lost fullness, and there was a constant slight furrow of harassment at the point where the top of her nose merged into her brow. She was not exactly more amiable in her manner towards me, but vague—as if I did not really impinge very much on her consciousness, as if I were some faintly disagreeable entity on the fringes. The time for me to leave the house was well past, but she did not refer to it, seeming in fact to have quite forgotten that there had ever been any question of my leaving. I kept out of her way as much as possible so that the sight of me should not remind her. The days passed and she said nothing and I began to lose my fear. All I had to do now, I felt, was get rid of the gardener and my life could follow its accustomed courses.

With this end in view I kept a close watch on the movements of Marion and the gardener but did not again succeed in surprising them together. They seemed, in fact, to have stopped meeting.

In the grounds he had worked to some effect on the periphery: he had clipped the hedges all the way round and along the front of the grounds where they abut on the road had cleared a belt of about fifty yards in length and a dozen in depth; also he had cleared the edges of the drive and reset the kerb stones and from among the trees he had collected dead wood, sawn it up and stacked it in one of the outhouses at the back. But the interior of the grounds, beneath which my tunnel lay, from the area of the pond back on the right side of the drive up to the beginning of the birches, was a wilderness still; now at the height of its tangled luxuriance, its summer apotheosis. Within this area the germination was almost overpowering. Bees tumbled madly about among the convolvulus, the great swathes of honeysuckle, the bramble flowers; blue and orange dragon-flies darted over the vivid green weeds at the edge of the pond; briar and bramble shoots lay athwart one's path with thorns like arrowheads often concealed in tangles of grass and willowherb and cow parsley, while underlying this rankness, like a reminder of a more elegant epoch, one was aware at times of Howard's cultivation, rose and magnolia and peony continued to flower, and from the herb garden, invaded now by chickweed and dandelion, the indomitable odours of mint and lavender added to the effluvium.

I continued to spend certain parts of each day crouched in my corner of the grounds with the field-glasses, perpetually harassed by small clouds of flies, straining to watch through whortleberry and hazel the activities of the woman in the bungalow. In the heat she wore loose dresses insecurely attached and nothing of much opacity beneath, so that for considerable periods I was racked between divining and seeing her nudity. Once when she was standing on a chair, cleaning her large front window, perhaps it was something to do with the glass against which she was standing, or perhaps she had indeed omitted to wear underclothes—it being so hot and she so far from the road—I was able swooningly to discern through her white dress a pubic darkness. That was a highlight, of course.

Also I watched the young robins, fledged now, cheeping and fluttering about in the hedge near the nest, with the thrushlike striations down the breast which showed their immaturity. There were still only four of them. I never did find out what had become of the fifth. My hide was still in position and I should have liked to study their feeding patterns now they were out of the nest, but the gardener was always somewhere about and I could never really relax sufficiently.

At the end of the week, on the Sunday afternoon, the gardener brought a friend to the house. I did not see them arrive, but when I emerged on to the drive at the side of the lawn I saw the three of them—the gardener, Audrey and another man— having tea on the terrace. My first instinct was to pass on down the drive, affecting not to have seen them—I knew that Audrey would acquiesce quite gladly in that course of action—but it was too great a departure from the normal; I had to know what it meant, moreover I was properly dressed for once, so I stopped and looked across and smiled, and smiled again and waved until my sister was obliged to smile back and as soon as she did this I went up the steps on to the terrace.

'Josiah, of course, you know,' Audrey said, in her most patrician tones. Her face was very flushed. 'And this is Josiah's friend, Mr Cade, this is my brother.' I did not offer to shake hands, such contacts are distasteful to me, but I nodded with a benign intention. The young man's face did not appear to have adapted itself yet to the presence of a fourth person. Nothing at all had happened on that face during my appearance on the terrace and the introduction and my sociable response. It had regarded me solemnly, indeed rather grimly. 'How do you do?' it said now. A long big-nosed face with very definite features, a curiously bloodless-looking mouth, steady grey eyes. He was sitting stiffly, but not in any apparent discomfort, in one of the basket chairs my sister had deemed appropriate for the terrace. His body was thick and square-shouldered. There was an undeniable power and even authority in his posture, in the way that, by refusing to recline in his chair, he rejected it and us all. He was several years older than Josiah.

'I was just remarking to Josiah, as we came down your drive,' he said, in a rather harsh voice, with an indefinable accent, clipped and Northern but difficult to identify precisely, 'it must be very satisfying, in this day and age, to have your own private park.' It was difficult to know whether this was intended seriously. His face did not relax when he spoke nor when his remark was greeted by my sister with fluttering, unnatural laughter. 'What a quaint way to describe it,' she said, and I should have known by this remark, even if there had been no other indications, that she was inwardly disarranged, not properly in control: to criticise the mode of expression of such a person was a major blunder, even if, as now became apparent, she disliked him.

He looked at her deliberately and she at him. She was still flushed and wore the remnants of that false merriment still on her face, and the antagonism between them was suddenly palpable. Then he looked away at Josiah and smiled, showing discoloured teeth. 'Quaint,' he said. 'That's a good word. There's enough land here for a housing estate.' The gardener smiled back immediately. I had not believed him capable of so much animation. His blue eyes glittered and he was looking at all our faces in turn.

'Isn't this land then?' Mr Cade said, indicating the area behind him by jerking his head. 'Aren't you the proprietor of it?'

'It's only an oversized garden really,' Audrey said. She had stopped smiling herself now, and her face looked blank as though at some private consternation. It was funny really, difficult to avoid smiling when I thought of how Audrey must have reacted in the first place to the suggestion of entertaining this person to tea. Oh yes, that is a nice idea Josiah, by *all* means ask your friend for Sunday, I should *very* much like to meet him. You assumed of course that some awed, deferential little creature would turn up, to whom you could have dispensed largesse, consolidating at the same time your influence over the gardener. How could you have envisaged any friend of his capable of disparaging you? Capable, moreover, of this sustained disparagement which compels you to be explicit in denying the very pretensions you had hoped over the tea cups so graciously to convey. Really it was funny. . . .

'Snakes,' the gardener's friend said in his harsh voice. 'Aren't you the gentleman who told Josiah there were deadly snakes hereabouts in large numbers?' For a moment or two I did not realise that he was speaking to me. Then I was thrown into considerable confusion, and did not know how to reply.

'That's right,' Josiah said. 'Small but deadly snakes you said, particularly in the shrubbery, you said.'

'There are no snakes in this type of country,' Mr Cade said, rather derisively it seemed to me. 'It is too much frequented.'

'Too much *what?*' Audrey said. 'What is this about snakes, Simon? Anyway, never mind, what I really wanted to ask you Mr Cade is whether you realise that Josiah is a very talented young man. With training and encouragement I think he could be a considerable artist. I know something about these matters and I give that as my definite opinion.'

'You're talking about this horse he gave you,' Mr Cade said. 'If I'm not mistaken.'

'Oh, you know about that do you? You told your friend about the horse then, Josiah?'

'He tells me everything,' Mr Cade said. He was looking at me now and I realised at this moment that if he knew Josiah had given Audrey the horse, he must know that I had suggested it in the first place. It was a very painful moment for me. He said nothing more, however, and after a moment or two, Audrey went on: 'I hope you will help him too, as far as you can. I know how much he listens to you. . . .' She was speaking now with an obvious attempt at appeasement. Mr Cade's knowledge must have come as a shock to her too. 'I myself,' she said, 'am prepared to give him every assistance and I think that, under my guidance of course, he could develop and broaden his talent, I am hoping that he will get enough work together to hold an exhibition. I have important friends in the district. . . .'

Mr Cade at this point threw back his head and with a quite extraordinarily malevolent expression, between a smile and a sneer, said, 'A spot of private patronising, such as occurred in the Renaissance.'

Before I could decide whether this was a genuine mistake, or a subtle way of rebuking Audrey's pretentiousness, Josiah started speaking and with such eagerness that it was clear that only pride in his friend had kept him silent so long: 'That is him all over, using all them kind a words, he has a tremendous vocabulary, well you would want a dictionary to keep up with him, you should hear him sometimes on the stall. . . .' He looked from face to face as he was speaking, with great concentration, reminding me of a dog that Howard used to keep, a spaniel named Phoebe, which used to scan our faces with similar intensity wherever there was some prospect of being taken for a walk. Josiah wanted to see, on Audrey's face and mine, our sense of the marvellousness of Mr Cade. What he saw on mine I don't know; he saw on my sister's a depreciating smile, an acid thinning of the lips. Mr Cade's sneering tone and Josiah's open admiration of him had overtaxed her conciliatory powers, always rather meagre. 'Well-educated people,' she said, 'express themselves as simply as possible, Josiah, they try to *communicate*, not just to impress. And in that way they avoid mistakes. Mr Cade must mean *patronage.*'

It was obvious that the gardener failed to understand her words, only the critical, disparaging intention. He must have understood, however, in that moment that the visit was not being a success. His face lost its animation, he glanced quickly and almost furtively at his friend, as though wanting to take a line from him, some clue as to how to behave. It suddenly struck me as quite unbelievable that four persons such as we were could be assembled on a terrace on a summer afternoon. 'Well,' I said, 'if you'll excuse me,' smiling and nodding, putting my hands on my thighs preparatory to getting up. But Cade abruptly stood up before I could do so. 'I have to be going now myself,' he stated.

'Oh, must you?' Audrey said.

He ignored this. Standing, he looked very tall. In his dark grey suit, with his large, rather clumsy face, his stiffness of bearing, he looked strangely like a man in plain clothes off duty, a prison warder perhaps or an orderly in a mental hospital —he looked quite capable of managing the difficult ones, holding them frothing indefinitely in a half-Nelson. He moved deliberately and with a complete absence of grace or flexibility. It was difficult to imagine him taking part in any games or sports or indulging in any physical frolicking whatever. There was something both absurd and sinister about him. His movement took him slightly in front of me and half turned away, and I was immediately troubled by a vague sense of recognition of something previously seen or dreamed.

He nodded briefly to me and then to Audrey, said 'Thank you very much Mrs Wilcox,' then he and Josiah crossed the terrace side by side, one ponderous and unswerving, his large head held firmly erect, the other narrow-hipped and lithe, taking quick short steps. They were like mastiff and whippet.

I glanced at Audrey. With slightly compressed lips she was

watching them leave together, and only later did it occur to me that she was consciously at that moment witnessing her own defeat, to be seen simply in the naturalness and apparent inevitability of their two forms together as they walked away. I did not understand this at the time, did not sense the terrible importance that all this had assumed for Audrey.

No, whatever signs there were in her face I failed to notice them because in the few moments before the two of them were lost to sight I had finally identified the thing that had been puzzling me. That set of the head, that tank-like forward motion—I knew now when I had seen it before: that was the figure in the distance, the figure I had seen receding down the road that afternoon when I heard the gate closing, when I had seen the gardener returning down the drive with a white, sick face.

Josh ...

MORTIMER SAYS THAT all Mrs Wilcox is interested in is my male member. His own words. She is missing the chopper, he says, since her old man snuffed it, anyone but you would see that a mile off. There is the art books, I tell him, that she is always showing me, and she says she will arrange an exhibition, you heard her say that yourself. I know what sort of exhibition she is thinking of, he said. She took a big interest in me, I said, since I gave her that horse. A course I know what he means, I wasn't born yesterday, but in my opinion Mrs Wilcox is genuinely interested in artistic things, as usual I didn't get no chance to explain this to Mortimer because he does not like her. That is all a pretext, he said. Do you really think, he said, that she is interested in the pilgrim soul in you and the sorrows of your changing face? Define your terms, I said to him, but he took no notice. She is only after the one thing, he said, before her fanny dries up altogether, but she doesn't like to admit it because she is old enough to be your mother and because you are just a scrubber, in her eyes though not in mine, so she goes on about art to conceal her motivations. (I am giving you his own words now.)

A course, Mortimer doesn't like her. He never liked her before, even before that time he come for tea and she started laying the law down. Right from the time she asked me how old I was he never liked her. And the way she spoke when she caught me with Marion that time, Mortimer thought it was overbearing, that was the word he used. He come back to that topic next time I seen him. Me, I seen nothing wrong in it, she was paying me for my time. But Mortimer saw it different. She wasn't hiring your male member, he said, though I have no doubt whatsoever that she'd like to. You are taking it for granted, he said, that she has the right to tell you where to sow your oats. When you say nothing wrong you mean nothing to conflict and obstruct their hypocritical bourgeoisie outlook, that is what you mean, Josiah. Don't you know, he said, that in this day and age all authority is being questioned? It was the same when you were working on the stall, letting old Mrs Morris order you about, do you want to be just one of the exploited masses? I have told you time and time again. In this day and age, people taking no notice of the Archbishop of Canterbury and all the Royal Dukes, let alone Mrs Wilcox, rebellion leaping out all over the place and you go round as if it was still the feudalism era.

Well, when he put it like that I could see it. I certainly did not want to be just one of the typical exploited masses, specially since I could see from the expression on Mortimer's face that he personally didn't have no time for them. Besides, he said, that was sexual jealousy. He knew she had come and apologised like, because I told him.

On the Thursday it was, just when I was finishing. Could I speak to you for a few minutes in the house? she said. We went into the same room we went before, but there wasn't no art books this time. I want to apologise to you, she said, as soon as we got in there. The way I spoke to you on Saturday, she said. It was quite unpardonable. She was talking as if she was out of breath, breathing in like at the same time, so the words seemed to go back into her, and straightaway I got this feeling that I always get these days when I am talking to her, that it wasn't real, as if these words belonged to a different occasion, or to some other people. That's all right, I said. I should of been getting on with the job.

No, she said, I don't mean in that way. She had lipstick on, that same bright red kind which is not good for her because she hasn't got much colour in her face like. And big green earrings. Her eyes are the nicest thing about her, long and narrow and sort of greenish-blue. She was wearing a white blouse that was styled like a man's shirt but with short sleeves. The insides of her arms was dead white, with the veins showing. I don't mean in that way, she said. Won't you have a seat? She pointed to the sofa. Perhaps you'd like a sherry, she said. She poured it out in the same kind of glasses—I never drank out of glasses like them before or since. Then she come and sat down beside me on the sofa. I don't mean as your employer, she said. I like to think that now a different kind of relationship has been established between us. The smell of sherry come off her in waves and that was before she even put this glass to her mouth like. She must have been on it all the afternoon. We have come to know each other well, in the course of these past weeks, she said. Don't you think so? Yes, I said. Yes, I do. She moved about a bit on the sofa beside me. Well, she said, it is as a friend . . . Although we are of different stations, she said. In the eyes of the world I mean. . . . She turned her face to look at me, I could see the lipstick shining on her mouth, and them eyes of hers looking at me very close, so close I had to look back into them and it was then I got a nasty shock because I wasn't there at all. What I mean is, she wasn't looking at me at all and this really give me the creeps because it reminded me of that bloke in the pub who nearly bashed me up just for asking for a shandy, he looked at me like that while he was squeezing my arm, looking at something very close or very far away, I dunno which. And I knew in that moment why I always felt our conversations wasn't real, it is because Mrs Wilcox don't live completely in this world. That is the only way I can think of putting it. Feelings like that come over me very strong, well I am psychic, what it amounts to, and it really give me a turn.

Only fools and weaklings follow the dictates of the world, she said, her own words, looking straight through me. And I have set you down as neither the one nor the other, Josiah.

I couldn't think of nothing to say to that. I could of asked her to define her terms a course, but I didn't like to. I finished the sherry in my glass and I put the glass down very careful like. Then I stood up. You're not going already? she said. Have some more sherry. No thank you, I said. I'll have to be going. I started off for the door before she could say any more. As a matter a fact I was scared. I was hoping we could have a long talk, she said. She was just behind me. Are you going out somewhere tonight? she said. I'll be seeing Mortimer, I said, when he comes off the stall. Oh yes, she said. That great friend of yours. I didn't say any of the things I was intending to, she said. Be wary of these girls, Josiah, you will find yourself trapped for life. Right, I said, I'll be on the look-out. And I started off up the drive.

Well, as I say, Mortimer knew all this, not in so much detail like, because he wouldn't listen to parts of it at all. It is a funny thing, he will sometimes listen to you and express it all better than you could yourself, other times he don't want to know. He don't usually want to know what I think about people, my opinion of them like. When I tried to tell him about Mrs Wilcox living partly in a different world and the way she looked and all, he said it was just that her eyes were glazed. She sits about all day, he said, soaking up the sherry and thinking about getting it, no bloody wonder her eyes have a funny look. Well, that is not it a course, but I didn't argue. Some things I know and Mortimer doesn't, he has a masculine intelligence but I am more the intuitive type myself.

How is Lionel these days? I asked him, very casual like. Getting on all right, is he? Oh yes, he said, Lionel's all right. Is Lionel one of the exploited masses? I said. No, he said. Lionel is not part of anything, he lives in his own cave. I dunno what you mean by that, I said. Well, he exists at a lower level, Mortimer said. It would be no good going on to him about being exploited, the question does not arise. You have to have people with a sense of human solidity, before you can exploit them.

Oh, I said, I see you been studying him like.

How is Maid Marion these days? he said. You have been silent of late on that score, Josiah. She is all right, I said. Yes, he said, you have been keeping reticent about it, positively incommunicado, are you getting it away then? Yes, I said, but that was a lie, a course, because I wasn't, not in them days. I wasn't far off it, mind.

You are on to a good thing there, Mortimer said. He started smiling. You ought to share her out, he said. How can you share somebody out? I asked him, making a joke of it like. You can't divide a person up, I said. I know which bit you'd keep if you could, he said. No, I mean pass her round. He was still smiling, his eyes going right back into his head and I smiled too, keeping him company like, not that I could see anything funny in it. Like the Communists do? I said, because I suddenly remembered some bloke telling me the Communists went in for that, all sharing together like. Free love, he said it was. It wasn't in Russia though, it was a place where there was swamps and the people lived in these long houses built up on poles, a lot of families together, and you could have any of the women in that house, they can all have any of the women.

Mortimer started laughing when I said that, which is something he almost never does. It made me think maybe that bloke was having me on. Mortimer has a little kind of barking laugh. Yes, he said, yes, that's right Josiah, just like the Communists.

Simon ...

THE VERY NEXT afternoon I found out where Marion and the gardener were meeting. It happened quite by accident, really. I was actually in the conservatory when I saw Marion go along the side of the house in the direction of the outhouses at the back. I happened to be standing motionless there because I had just been witnessing an extraordinary thing. The conservatory, which is built against the wall at the back of the house, though in Howard's day crammed with plants, and humid, now conserves nothing much except dry soil in pots and the odour of desiccation. All seemed much as usual as I was passing through. There is a large resident spider which I have named Joey and I saw the murderous fawn tips of his legs as he lurked in the cavity of the window frame where the putty has crumbled away: it is an adroit fly that survives one of Joey's rushes. Several of the panes are missing, a daddy-long-legs had got in through one of them and was now blundering round, presumably trying to get out again. I stopped to watch, wondering if it would have the misfortune to alight anywhere near Joey. Three times it went round, bumping into things, its silly stilts hanging down in a bunch, thin wings whirring. Then a bright yellow wasp flew in, the sound of it filled the place until by design or accident it collided with the daddy-long-legs and in complete silence fell with it to the paved floor. They embraced, lay together for a moment or two and then the extraordinary thing happened: the wasp nipped or bit off each of the other creatures legs about half way up. Methodically. After which it flew up and out as unerringly as if it had been able to smell the exit. The daddy-long-legs, unable now to launch itself, began to gyrate slowly on its stumps. I was watching these gyrations, wondering what refinement could have led the wasp to maim without killing, when I saw Marion go past not a dozen yards away.

If she had turned her head she would certainly have seen me. Her face bore a calm or rather a *heedless* look, as though her immediate surroundings could have no conceivable interest for her; an expression, it was to strike me later, in its dreamy self-absorption, very like that of the goddess on the wall of my subterranean salon; not at all a saintly or self-abnegating expression, of course. (I could never have on my wall any head that a halo might suit.) She passed along by the conservatory, but instead of turning left towards the outhouses she continued straight on, across the paved area, down the narrow earth path that runs for a few yards between ragged privet hedges. I waited a little—perhaps it was some trifling errand—perhaps she would soon reappear. Then, pausing only to put an end to the daddy-long-legs' predicament, I went out of the conservatory and along to the beginning of the path. There was no sign of her. She must have passed through the gate into the orchard. I lost no more time, but went quickly down the path and through the gate. She was nowhere to be seen among the apple trees. For a few moments I stood there, rather at a loss. The orchard is on high ground; beyond it, falling away gradually to distant villa gardens and the sea, there is open arable country quite devoid of cover except for a small copse some five or six hundred yards off in a declivity between two fields. She could not have reached the copse in this short while. Then the only possible explanation came to me: one of the fields that lies between the orchard and the copse runs level for about fifty yards, then slopes quite steeply, levelling out again, at its lower end; Marion must be in this dip, invisible to me from here—dead ground as I have heard it called. Sure enough, a few minutes later she emerged on to the more gradually sloping ground. I watched her cross this and the next field and disappear into the copse.

I could not follow her directly, of course, as I should be in full view the whole way. However I know the terrain well, having two years previously spent a good deal of time watching the courtship of magpies there. The copse itself continues the downward slope of the field at first, and in its central part, where the birches give way to hawthorn, there is a shallow dip in the ground, much overgrown, in which at some time various unwanted household goods have been dumped, and from here the ground begins to rise again and the copse thins, ending at a ragged hedge which serves as a line of demarcation for the field beyond. Standing there, I worked it out: first of all retreat to the orchard, then a wide encircling movement, bringing me to the hedge lower down, where I could pass through it and so approach the copse under its cover.

It took me twenty-two minutes by my wrist watch. The slowest bit was the last, working my way along the hedge until I was directly behind the copse. Once there, however, I had a splendid view. Because of the rising ground I could see clear over the hollow into the bushes beyond, and the upper branches of the birch trees. I could detect no sound or movement anywhere in the copse; nothing stirred in there except the occasional gauzy glint of an insect's wing. Below me in the hollow, enmeshed with peculiarly lush grass as if they in some way nourished the roots, were fretted buckets, soup tins, the carcase of a pram; reminding me suddenly, as I relaxed after my exertions, of that remote refuse of childhood one seemed to stumble on when one was quite alone, always in slightly fearsome places, hollows, the banks of cuttings, dried stream beds. Places of intense loneliness and stealth. A bluebottle buzz, the sweet trickle of a bird's song, my beating heart, the wonder at my own existence rooting me there until I was compelled to some violent physical movement. . . .

No sound or movement from the copse. They are lying concealed somewhere among the bushes beyond the hollow.

I move very cautiously several yards to my right, still nothing. Back again and then further in the other direction, looking steadily through the lower part of the hedge and I am beginning to think there is no one there at all when quite suddenly I see their legs. The gardener's trouser cuffs I can see and his maroon socks and the narrow sole of one shoe; Marion's white leg from the middle of the calf downward, but only that one leg, the other must be raised. Her shoe is hanging off at the heel, with an effect curiously sluttish yet childish too. They are lying turned to each other as it appears. The feet of neither make the smallest movement—it is as though they are asleep.

Asleep or in some toils: it is with a definite sense that they are imprisoned here in the copse, prisoners of each other and of me, that I begin very cautiously to withdraw.

Josh ...

MARION AND ME done it, the whole thing. I always knew I would get it out of sight before I was twenty-one. We done it twice, inside an hour, and I was ready, I could of done it again, only she said no, Mrs Wilcox will be up and about now, we got to go. So you could count it as three times really. Well, I dunno if you could count the first one, matter a fact, because I was not exactly in her. I didn't have no time. I was there, I was there all right, but I never got it in. I think you could count it though. I mean, there was *contact*. Anyway, I am going to tell Mortimer three. The trouble with the first one was I couldn't find it in time. That might sound funny, we all know it is right there between their legs and anyway I had my hand on it just a second before, but that is the fact, I couldn't find it, not the way in I mean. (A course I will not tell Mortimer I couldn't find the way in.) I didn't have enough time, that was the main trouble. I only just had the time to get away from her and turn my back before it come shooting out a yard off into the grass. I dunno if I made any noise but she knew what was happening, she knew, she put an arm round me very tight, round my shoulder and she held on all the time I was coming, she's got some strength for all she's thin.

Why did you do that? she asked me. Well, I said, I couldn't hold it in, thinking she meant why did I let go so quick like, but, No, she said, I don't mean that, I mean why did you turn your back on me? You can turn back round now, she said, at any rate. It was as if you were ashamed, she said. Why did you?

Well I couldn't find no answer, only it seemed natural at the time, when I felt it coming like. I dunno, I said. I dunno why. I turned back round and looked at her face, which was the same as ever a course, but kind of bare-looking, and I was surprised in a way it looked the same and I wondered if my face looked any different to her. Hers wasn't exactly the same either, not when you really looked, she seemed more sure of things than I ever seen her look before. And she spoke in a tone a voice as if she was sure. You needn't have turned away, she said. It's because you have been on your own so much that you did that. You're not used to sharing, are you? she said, and just for a second I thought of that conversation with Mortimer. You have never done this with a girl before, have you? she said. She knew, it was no use me trying to cover it up, she knew from me not being able to find the way in and then turning my back like. A course I could of told her that I had done it before, but I didn't, I didn't say nothing, and she smiled, a real happy smile. You needn't have done that, she said, and I hope you won't do it again. Smiling all the time but not as if she'd found me out, not that sort of smile, just looking glad that it was so.

Lucky for me Mrs Wilcox found us in the grounds that day. I would never of got so far with Marion if we hadn't of started meeting in a lonelier kind of place. . . .

There was buttercups growing in the fields and I picked a few on my way to meet her. Then when I got there I started just for a joke to test if she liked butter. You hold the buttercup against a person's throat and see if it makes a sort of yellow glow on the throat. It all depends on if you got the sun behind you or not. So she put her head back and closed her eyes and I put the buttercup against her throat. Well, she said, do I like butter or not? But I didn't say nothing, I kissed the place on her throat where the buttercup was shining yellow and I kept my mouth there, I could feel the pulse in her throat beating right inside my mouth, and she let herself lie back and my hand went straight between her legs, she never tried to stop me like she always had before, just sort of moaned a bit when she felt me touching her there, then she was wriggling to get under me, I didn't waste no time getting her worked up like they always say you're supposed to, I was in too much of a hurry and besides she didn't need it. Then I couldn't get it in her, not that time. You don't ever need to do that again, she said. Turning your back like that.

The second time was better. What I mean is, you could really count the second time. I got it right in. As soon as I got it in I started coming again, but this time a lot slower, it took quite a long time to come and all that time I was moving inside her and she was making sort of little noises like it was hurting.

After that I fell asleep for a bit. When I woke up she was looking down at me still with the same kind of happy look. She had her back to the sun and her hair all round her head was bright with the sunshine and I couldn't look at her for long because of the brightness but I know no one but me had been there before, so what Mortimer said about the way she walked was just not appliable and I made up my mind right there and then to tell Mortimer I done it three times and to tell him he was wrong about Marion's way of walking.

Simon ...

I HAD NOT intended to say anything to my sister at this stage, keeping the revelation of these trysts as a trump card so to speak. But events forced my hand.

When I reached the grounds again the first thing I heard was Audrey's voice calling: 'Jo—osh . . . Jo—osh . . . Jo—si—aah!' There was in this call a certain teasing note, deliberately infused to avoid any imputation of urgency. And the oftener Audrey had to repeat the call, the more, that is, it became apparent that the gardener was not within earshot, the more pronounced this archness grew. It did not stop however, dry up for lack of response as any truly casual summons would. No. It went on, wilful, self-deprecating, terribly obstinate. Jo—si—aah! Loud enough to be heard anywhere in the grounds, it was not loud enough for those two lying embraced in the copse to hear.

Rounding a bend in the drive I came upon her just after she had uttered yet another cry. She was standing near the kerb and seemed to be listening, her head rather stiffly inclined. Her expression was serious, reflecting nothing of that facetiousness of tone. It came to me again, seeing her standing there with her head cocked like a thrush on a lawn, that Audrey was losing her mental balance. I wondered too at the extraordinary fruits our actions bear: how could Audrey, going armed in righteousness to the Labour Exchange to declare that a vacancy existed, have known that not much afterwards she would be discovered somewhat distraught in a driveway calling repeatedly on a name?

She straightened up when she saw me but did not speak. 'You will not find him here,' I said. I looked into her face with what boldness I could muster, for I had decided in this moment to force the issue, take advantage of having caught Audrey calling out in loneliness.

'What do you mean?' she said. 'Are you feeling all right Simon?' 'I'm quite well,' I said. It was true however that I was having some difficulty in controlling my excitement now that I had decided on this bold stroke. The episode during the garden party must be still rankling in her mind; if I could now show her what was happening in the copse I might bring about a revulsion against the gardener great enough to result in his dismissal, thus removing all threat to my tunnel and in all probability causing Audrey to turn to me for comfort and support—I am after all her brother. Failure, of course, would be disastrous, as Audrey would merely redouble her animosity towards me, probably recall her threat to turn me out. It was enough to make anybody feverish.

'You won't find him anywhere in these grounds,' I said.

She seemed to make a brief effort to look enquiring, then her face slackened. 'He's gone then has he?' she said quietly and I was amazed at the readiness with which she supplied this explanation of my words.

'Gone,' I said. 'No, he hasn't gone. Why should you think that?'

'You cannot confine a free spirit.' For a moment or two after you utter these extraordinary words I look at you in silence. There is something complacent in your expression, proclaiming how well you know the temperament of this boy. It is what you have always wanted, Audrey, I suppose, the role of foster mother and artistic adviser combined, power and good taste, the satisfaction of superior discrimination; sexual education no doubt also to be taken in hand as occasion presents—I see now for the first time that the gardener was sent especially to entrap you. From the gift of the horse you were lost. From the gift of the horse. . . . For a few moments, as I look into your tired face, that small complacency gone already, lines of anxiety and strain returned, I feel compunction. Even sorrow. It is hard to be denied ambition for another human being, even harder than for oneself, and of course you wish this youth well.... But this is a question of my tunnel, of my survival. I harden my heart and proceed: 'I am not sure what you mean by that, Audrey, but he is quite near home. Would you like me to show you where he is grazing currently?'

She nods her head slowly, like a reluctant child. Her personality and indeed the entire relationship between us seem to have changed in these few minutes, and I experience an access of power and confidence. 'If you follow behind me I will show you,' I promise her and again she nods her head wordlessly. We pass round the house, she about six paces docilely behind me. But we have hardly got beyond the orchard when I am invaded by another feeling, my triumph takes on further intensity, and this is because after all these years I am taking Audrey along a Secret Pathway.

Secret Pathways were very important to me when I was a small child, because I was convinced at that time that there was a richer, more exciting mode of being lying on the immediate confines of the one I actually experienced; near but unattainable, because I had failed to locate any of the entrances. Any gate, any gap in the hedge might lead to it, if only one knew. I believed that if I could find an entrance my life would be quite changed. This belief was very strong and I have sometimes thought that my tunnelling might be an attempt to construct such a pathway for myself, to thread, as it were, my delights together. However that may be, Audrey succeeded early in discovering my belief in this more vivid parallel life and she played on it. She claimed to know where the Secret Pathway was and I believed her—I was too young to conceive duplicity on that scale. I suppose I was five years old. Whenever there was cover, the chance of concealment, she would depart, with some casual remark for others but a meaning look for me so that I knew with immediate anguish that she was

about to enter the Secret Pathway at some neighbouring
accession point. She was always fleeter than I, so that if I
attempted to pursue her, I would before many moments be
left alone among alien herbage, torn by brambles, stung by the
whip back of branches, blinded and choked by my exertions
and my tears. I used to call after her, begging her to show me
the secret way, but she never did; she never even promised
she would; and that is what chiefly surprises me now, her
extremely pitiless guarding of this secret. After some time she
would reappear, lacerating me further by her triumphant
complacency of manner. . . .

Now she walked behind me as we left the orchard on our
right and reached the edge of the field. The roles were reversed
but I at least was willing to share my knowledge. . . . Suddenly,
however, she spoke and I knew from the tone and volume that
she was no longer following. 'I'm going back, Simon,' she
said. 'I don't really know why I followed you this far. I don't
know what we are doing here, the pair of us.'

She had stopped and stood there regarding me with dazed
enquiry, as though recently roused from sleep.

'Oh,' I said, 'but you can't go back now. It is not much
farther.' Useless to protest of course. And now perhaps un-
necessary: despite my disappointment I sensed that during
these few minutes she had absorbed the knowledge of what
she would see, in the way that one perceives good or evil, by
a sort of assimilation. At any rate she asked no more questions
but turned on her heel and began to walk back through the
long grass, back towards the orchard. She had summoned a
sort of pride.

Her going left me undecided. There did not seem much
point in returning alone to the copse. After hesitating for some
minutes I began to make my way back to the grounds. As I was
nearing the side of the drive I heard the scraping whirr of the
gate. I had only just time enough to get back among the bushes
before Major Donaldson passed along the drive carrying a
bunch of red carnations and looking, as it seemed to me, less

than his usual self. I say this because his face wore a pinched reverential expression as though all the jolliness had been squeezed out through the corners of his eyes and mouth, somehow reducing in the process the total surface area. I did not follow him, but remained where I was, waiting.

It must have been an hour at least. I sat down among the bushes and part of the day wheeled over me as I waited. At first I thought of them, Major Donaldson and Audrey sitting together, conducting some conversation, the Major crossing, uncrossing, recrossing his grey flannels, Audrey touching her opal brooch, the carnations glowing prominently in the place where she had put them. Marion, still warm from her sporting in the copse, in silent attendance on them. Or would Marion be *de trop*? Was the Major, could he conceivably be, laying his life before Audrey, taking her hand in his? A Mrs Donaldson there was not, nor ever had been, as far as anybody knew. But this thought was too improbable to be entertained, or entertained for long, and in dismissing it, I dismissed Audrey and the Major too, at least for the time being, and I began in a drowsy way to think of the woman at the bungalow sweeping her front, hanging out the washing, cleaning the windows. The truth was I suddenly began to feel very tired, quite exhausted in fact, with all the excitement I had been going through, all these alarums and excursions, the sheer nervous strain of watching everything, maintaining a constant vigilance and striving always to fit everything that happened into a *design*. Heavy work for a mortal man, best left to the Supreme Author of course—but in this tiny part of the terrain I wanted to be in on it too, since it affected me so much more immediately than it could conceivably affect Him.

Clouds formed and darkened, shutting out the sun. Far over to my right, beyond the bungalow and the wheat, over the broom and ferns that marked the beginning of the hills, an area characterised by space and rapine, a sparrow-hawk loitered high in the sky, dipped, rose again. At my feet was a plant with denticulated leaves one of which was not dark green like the others but a beautiful soft crimson. Now why this alchemy for this particular leaf? No doubt it was some impoverishment, some weakness in the veins to which it owed this beauty. Definitely a moral in it somewhere. . . .

Then I heard their steps on the drive. They came into view walking side by side a yard or so apart, neither of them speaking. My sister's face had the haggard look it had been showing lately and the Major still seemed curiously abashed. They looked like a couple who have just been tediously and inconclusively quarrelling. I was able by moving a few yards up through the shrubbery, to see them pause at the gate for a few moments. I saw the Major smile, decline his head, turn away. He squared his shoulders before he started walking as if he was marching into a future, no doubt beset with difficulties, but at any rate free from the interview just conducted.

My sister stood alone at the gate for a couple of minutes, watching him depart, presumably. Then she set off back towards the house. She had not gone more than a dozen paces, however, before she stopped dead again and began a series of actions at first inexplicable, a sort of bracing and relaxing of the body as though engaged in some kind of breathing exercise. Had I been near enough to hear the sounds of course I should have known at once. I had not realised up till then how closely weeping is identified with its sounds, with bursts of noise, chokings, snifflings, gulpings, sobs. It was the sudden droop of her body, the declension of her whole form, that first alerted me. Her shoulders slumped forward, her arms hung straight down, nervelessly abandoned. Her head performed a rearing motion. Her face was quite expressionless. She was in the act of raising it. She tilted her face up, up, until she was looking over the trees into the sky, then as suddenly as a crack appears in glass her face crumpled and wrinkled, her lips drew back tightly over her teeth and her head began a slow inclination. Now indeed I sensed the sounds that must be accompanying all this—the short gasping inspirations followed by long sighs, irregular and painful owing to the partially closed glottis. Her lowered head remained stationary for a second or two, then began again its blind upward motion, up, up, the crumples ironed out again but the face wet now, higher and higher as if the source of tears lay somewhere up beyond the trees, somewhere in the darkening sky, as if she had to get her face at the correct angle to the universe before a fresh access could be achieved. As a spectacle it was fascinating.

Josh ...

I NEVER SHOULD of told Mortimer in the first place. Now I dunno what to do. It was just one time when I thought I caught him out like. He said you could tell by watching them walk. Well, I said to him, that is not the case with Marion, it is not appliable. And I told him we done it three times. It was true in a way a course, but he took me up on it. Three times, he said, she would not have let you in three times if she was not used to the chopper, she would have been too sore, Josiah. Besides, he said, what is sexual intercourse?

I thought he would of been glad. But he took the point of view of a realist. As soon as I finished telling him he started taking the realist point of view. What I didn't know then was that he had meant it, he had meant what he said about sharing. He had been meaning it all the time. What is sexual intercourse? he said, and he got the same look on his face as when we done that to the bird, before we done it, I mean, while we was talking, exactly the same, and the funny thing was I started feeling the same as I done before, sort of guilty and out of breath, before he even said anything, just from the look on his face and believe it or not I started getting a hard on again, not completely, it just went half stiff, then stopped. I ask you, he said. What is sexual intercourse, what does it consist of? A man and a woman having it, I said. That is only one aspect, he said. You are overlooking buggery and soddery, Josiah. There are people, he said, who regularly have sexual intercourse with a loaf of bread. Never mind, it is sufficient for our purpose. Now tell me,

is it brief or of long duration? It is brief, I said. Momentary, the
pleasure is momentary, he said. Is it minds or bodies that
perform it? Bodies, I said. Very well then, he said, it is one
organ achieving a degree of penetration into another organ,
that is all. Can you say it is more than that? I suppose not, I
said. In that case, he said, it doesn't matter whose organ it is,
does it? I suppose not, I said.

I will never forget that conversation with Mortimer, standing
there, watching his face, waiting for what was coming and
feeling sort of tightened up. We was standing against the
railing that runs along the promenade. Thursday night it was,
Mortimer's night off. About six, sun well down, they was
coming up off the beach with their deck chairs. If I were down
to my last crust, Mortimer said, I would share it with you, Josiah.
Well, I know that's true. Is it a go then? he said. What? I said.
You know, he said. Doing like the Communists, share and
share alike. You mean with Marion, I said. None other, he
said.

Well, I seen from his face that he meant it and a course
Mortimer never changes, once his mind is made up, you
will never find him wavering like, never. I thought it was
something to do with what I told him before, I thought I had
brought it all on myself by exaggerating like, so I started trying
to tell him what actually happened. As a matter a fact, I said,
we never done it three times. We only done it once and it hurt
her, I said. That is neither here nor there, he said. That is a
mere detail. I hope you are not going to take the sentimentalist
point of view, he said.

Just then one of the blokes working on the deck chairs
that I knew a bit come up to us and said he had run out of
fags. They was all coming in off the beach with their chairs
asking for their deposit money back so he didn't have no time
to go and buy a packet. Mortimer does not smoke a course,
but I give him one, and it give me time to think a bit. I said,
supposing she don't want to? But Mortimer only smiled. What
I was meaning was that it was not just a question of organs

and penetration, but Marion had a will of her own. Suppose she don't want to, I said. You just let me know, he said, the next time you are going down into the bushes with her, just you give me a bit of notice.

It was then I started feeling really scared. Up till then I had been thinking in the back of my mind, it don't matter, it don't mean nothing, Marion would never agree to such a thing. I mean, I think she was impressed with Mortimer's intellect and powers of conversation but she said to me several times he was not her type and she never liked it if I talked about Mortimer to her. But now I could see it did not make no difference whether she agreed or not.

But Mortimer, I said, if we done that we would have to get out. And I looked into his face, hoping to see he was having me on all the time, because I could swear on the Bible that the idea of it didn't have no appeal to me at all, them sort of things is not in my nature. Mortimer was looking very serious now. That's all right, he said. Time for a change anyway. You and me on the road together, Josiah, just the two of us together. The day after we do it we'll get off on the road, bright and early.

Just you and me? I said. Certainly, he said. Well, it was what I had always thought about, me and him travelling together, just the two of us. I even pictured what clothes we would be wearing, things like that. Well, I dunno, I said.

As a matter a fact there was another feeling growing up in my mind all this time, and that was *surprise*. The thing that Mortimer was suggesting was somehow or other surprising, I did not know why at the time, I only knew it wasn't what I would ever of expected of him, it didn't go with his character, not this particular thing. For instance when we done that to the bird there was nothing surprising in it at all, it was something that had to happen. But this was different.

Listen, Mortimer said, you have got to see things steadily and see them whole. It is only a corporeal question, he said. That is what you must get into your noddle, Josiah. If you take the philosophical view, he said (I am giving his own words now). And that is why I want you to be there and see it happening, so that you will be able to take the philosophical and realist view in future, and understand it is only organs. We will despatch into limbo, he said, all this romantic sludge. I dunno what you mean, I said. Define your terms. In any case, I said, I don't want to do it.

Oh, you don't, don't you? he said. Take Lionel now, there is a case in point. Oh yes, I said. Lionel is a realist, he said, after a fashion. He is leaving soon. Oh, I said, I didn't know that. Yes, he said, he is fed up with the stall and I cannot find it in my heart to blame him. He tried to fiddle a few bob the other day, and old Mrs Morris caught him out. Now he is feeling a bit disenchanted. He is going to Skegness where according to him the streets are paved with gold. He wants me to go with him. Oh yes, I said. Are you going then? I was trying to speak casual like, but my mouth got that numb feeling straight off, thinking about him and Lionel together.

Well I don't know really, Mortimer said. It depends on you. Then I saw what he meant, he would go with Lionel if I didn't agree to this other thing, and I knew in that moment that I had made a big mistake only telling Mortimer the facts about Marion and not trying to make him see her as a real person like. I should of told him more about her feelings, like the way she makes herself into two persons when she is having a bath, them sort of things. Then she would of been a real person to Mortimer like she was to me and he would not of had this idea.

Listen Mortimer, I started trying to say, but my face didn't feel like it belonged to me by this time, listen, you know one funny thing Marion said, she said how do the clouds keep the rain in? They must have skins, she said, or they couldn't keep the rain in. . . .

I was trying to catch up but a course it was no use, I should of been telling Mortimer these kind of things ever since I first met Marion. His face did not change at all, and all he said was,

You'd better make up your mind, Josiah.

I dunno what to do now. Last night after I left him I walked round for hours, thinking what to do. There is no one to ask.

Simon ...

IT MAY SEEM strange but I did not at that time associate Audrey's outburst of weeping with the Major's visit at all. I had seen knowledge in her face when she refused to follow me any further; and because I was myself occupied with the problem of ousting the gardener, I tended to relate my sister's behaviour to him. I thought simply that she had suppressed her feelings during the visit for propriety's sake and that immediately on the Major's departure they had risen to the surface.

It was not until some weeks afterwards when my sister was almost well again, though, of course, permanently disabled, that I learnt what the visit had been about. Audrey herself never once mentioned it though she proved willing enough to discuss other things that had happened during this period.

I had gone down to the Post Office to despatch some letters for Audrey, who though strong enough now to get about herself, still evinced a strong reluctance to appear in public; understandably enough, in view of her appearance and the rumours that had been circulating. So I used to go out and do these little errands for her. I met the Major while I was standing at the far end of the counter licking stamps and sticking them on the envelopes. We were both dressed in mackintoshes as the weather had turned rainy, and he wore in addition a fawn corduroy cap. It was the cap I became aware of first, hovering, as it were, beyond my right shoulder, then I detected the Major beneath it. 'How are you, *ugh, ugh*?' I said, immediately beginning to emphasise by a series of grimaces the unpleasant taste of the glue on the stamps. Such encounters are hurdles after all, at least they are so to me, one must get over them somehow, and the more activity generated, by gesture, grimace or contortion, the better and easier it all seems to go, by the time physical order has been restored, the encounter is over, people are saying farewell, hurrying off. Or so it seems to me. For this reason I made *moues* of distaste throughout the Major's opening remarks. He asked after Audrey and said how sorry and so forth and his eyes under the cap did not look happy. 'Yes,' I said, 'Yes, well . . . of course, it was to all of us, *ugh, ugh. . . .*'

'Stamps have a nasty taste, have they?' he said, very sympathetically as though it were part of the condolences. He stood by, coughing and touching his moustache while I finished the letters, then he accompanied me out on to the pavement. Here we stood for some minutes more.

'I feel myself partly responsible,' he said. 'To some extent that is. Just before your sister . . . some days before it happened, I had the unpleasant duty . . . as chairman of the committee. . . .' He looked sideways at me and I nodded and smiled a thin distasteful smile.

'Surely not,' I said.

'Yes, yes,' he said. 'I am still chairman.'

'No,' I said, 'I meant surely not responsible.'

'Well,' he said. 'She was very keen, we all know that. And of course had I known at the time how seriously she would take it. . . . The fact is, it fell to my lot to tell her that the producer wanted her out of the play. *Insisted*. Yes. No, she had no acting ability whatever. Not a scrap, you know. We had only just engaged the producer and we didn't want to upset him over the first play he was putting on, Ibsen's *Ghosts* it was, your sister was to have played Mrs Alving. The part was beyond her you know. Quite beyond her. I went along. . . . It fell to my lot to go along one afternoon and tell her. She didn't seem to take it too badly at the time. But it occurred to me afterwards you know, perhaps it weighed on her. . . .'

He looked at me again, almost furtively. He wanted to be told by me, the next of kin, that he was not to blame. I remember the squeezed look on his face as he went up the drive that day, holding the carnations. Why that look, as of someone breaking bad news, if he hadn't known how seriously she would take it. . . ? The committee had known perfectly well how much she minded, but had preferred to placate their producer, some small-time actor out of work, who would normally have been washing dishes at one of the hotels on the front. I had after all been fighting for my life, whereas the committee. . . .

'Well,' I said. 'What you told her probably had its effect.'

It occurred to me now that other people might well have been conducting a campaign against Audrey. Other than myself, I mean. How did I know for example that this visit of Major Donaldson, in the course of which he had destroyed my sister's dramatic ambitions, was not simply one stroke in a calculated series—the only one in which he had been detected? Looking now at his moustache, his full red lower lip—somewhat fuller than formerly with umbrage at the tone I had taken —it seemed to me likely enough that he had been machinating against Audrey. Perhaps Gravelin had too, and Dovecot and Miriam and even a person like Spink. Perhaps everybody was machinating against everybody else, by accident the attacks on my sister had been too concerted, she had succumbed.

'It must have seemed very ungrateful to her,' I said. 'Particularly after the way she had worked for your wretched—for the Dramatic Society, which I must say I thought exercised an, er, baneful, influence on her from the beginning. Don't forget the garden party, the way she organised that raffle. You would otherwise have had to hire a hall, Major Donaldson.'

'I am not likely to forget,' he said, in a tone which was now so full of anger that I felt frightened. Nevertheless I felt impelled to go on, mainly I think to allay my own feelings of guilt about Audrey but at least partly in repudiation of the Major's obvious belief that in such situations a gentleman does not gratuitously exacerbate another gentleman's bad conscience.

'And then to be cast off,' I said. 'Like an, er, old *boot. Ugh!* No, my dear Major, I'm afraid you must be held in part responsible. . . .'

This was only after all what he had begun by saying, but he gave me an outraged glare. 'Very well, sir,' he said. 'Very well.' And he turned on his back and went off at a spanking pace up the High Street.

This happened a good three weeks after the event. And so, that afternoon, watching the mystic obeisances of my sister's weeping, her wet, blind face, I attributed everything to her feelings about the gardener. This ignorance I urge in my turn as an extenuating circumstance. It was no part of my intention to drive Audrey to any desperate action. I wished only to ensure the dismissal of the gardener. . . .

Later that afternoon it rained quite heavily. Audrey remained in her room. There was no sign of Marion anywhere downstairs either. I wandered round the house rather aimlessly for a bit. I thought of going out into the grounds but it was still raining, a thin steady rain now, that showed no signs of abating. The gardener was nowhere about and I supposed he had gone home. I was thinking of going upstairs myself, when I heard voices from above. I went out into the passage that leads to the back of the house. I advanced a few paces towards the back stairs. From here the voices were louder, I could distinguish Audrey's sharp tones and Marion's more muted ones, but the words were impossible to make out. My sister's voice rose, fell, rose again. A door shut sharply. The voices stopped. I went hastily back into the drawing-room where I stood looking out through the french window at the rain. After a few minutes someone entered the room. I turned and it was Marion. She was very flushed and I saw after a moment that she was close to tears. Evidently Audrey had been upbraiding her. She smiled at me in her usual uncertain way and said she had left her knitting somewhere.

'What is the matter?' I asked her. I have a soft spot for Marion, though lately she has begun to horrify me rather;

the light-coloured clothes she wears have become associated in my mind with sacrifices and also grave linen. She has lain in the gardener's embrace, in her white dress, with her shoe dangling off. I cannot at all reconcile this image with her present one, flushed and weepy, bony-shouldered, looking for her knitting. She was also the creature in that charmed area of the bushes, lying there, the smoke from his cigarette curling up, the sun glossing the leaves. It suddenly brought home to me how inscrutable we human creatures are, what a mystery inheres in every follicle.

'What is the matter?' I said, but she only shook her head, and smiled again and went out.

Josh ...

I WALKED ROUND a long time, trying to think what I should
do. I couldn't think of nothing. The bloke with the bad hip
woke me up early, it was just getting light. He went back to
sleep again but I couldn't. I started thinking again. Then it
come to me all of a sudden that Mortimer might of been right
about her way of walking. I mean I argued with him and
contradicted him like because he said it in front of Lionel, he
was taking the piss. I didn't argue with him about her way of
walking, not really. It is not a thing you take a lot of notice
of anyway, not unless there is something special about it, like
a limp, say. But after I thought for a bit I seemed to remember
that Marion does walk with her knees turned out a bit. And if it
is really true what Mortimer said, and I got no reason to
disbelieve it except it seemed to hurt her when we done it, a
course she could of been putting that on. . . . If it is really
true then maybe it don't matter so much, I mean maybe it
would not matter so much to her. But why should she of been
putting it on? . . . Mortimer and Lionel off up the motorway,
off up to Skegness. He would turn Mortimer against me,
Mortimer would be sorry we was ever friends. . . . She *does*
walk funny, more I think of it. . . . No good saying she could of
had Plastic Surgery, she probably couldn't afford it, you can't
get it done on the National Health. . . . And why did she want
to go down there in the first place? Into them bushes. It was her
that suggested it. Asking for trouble. I might of been anybody.
That means she don't care who it is so long as she gets it and

that is just what Mortimer says. I see now that Mortimer is right. I can see it from the realist point of view it is just a question of organs. So long as I don't think about them eyes of hers looking at me, only at me, when she said she knew a place. . . . Mortimer will make me stay and watch, I know he will. Friday, three o'clock.

Simon...

THIS MORNING IS fresh and odorous after the rain in the night. Walking through the grounds I get the cuffs of my trousers stuck all over with wet grass seeds. There is a blackbird singing somewhere close by, as I take up my position in the corner of the grounds. Across the fields the bungalow sleeps. The early sun shines gently on its bow windows, gleams on its grey slate roof. The field between it and me is darkened with wet, thick with daisies and meadowsweet. Beyond is the great sweep of the cornfield, a uniform green-gold to the horizon now that the poppies and cornflowers have been submerged by the rising tide of wheat; the whole extent of it shimmers in the sunshine, simmers in the light wind, a spectacle of great beauty. From among and beyond it the songs of yellow hammers and larks tangling together so that individual accents are not distinguishable. Dove-grey clouds round the sun, thinning from moment to moment. It is going to be a glorious day.

The woman appears with her dear little brush and dustpan. I am ready with the field-glasses, focused beforehand of course, and for the next seven minutes and fifty-two seconds I am rapt.

Perhaps I am less than usually alert as I am leaving the place, certainly I hear nothing, nothing at all, but as I reach the edge of the drive I come practically face to face with the gardener's friend, Mr Cade, who is making his way fairly briskly towards the gate. I am taken completely by surprise, but he nods at me with what seems a genial intention. 'Grand morning,' he says. I cannot help looking down at his feet. He is wearing what are known or were known as *chukka boots*, grey suède with crêpe soles at least an inch thick—I see now why he made no sound on the drive. And the fronts of them, right up to the laces, are dark with wet.

'Indeed it is,' I reply, gesturing towards the morning from behind a privet bush. I still feel shaken by this unexpected meeting, particularly as I cannot understand how this person could have entered the grounds without my knowledge. 'If you want the gardener, er, Josiah,' I say, 'you had better go round to the other side. He is working there this morning.'

'No,' he says, regarding me steadily but without particular expression. A long, pale, big-chinned face. 'No, my business was with the lady of the house.'

He looks at me a while longer as though something is not clear to him and then sets himself forward in motion, a deliberate progress down the drive. I say good day to his retreating back, which shows no awareness of being thus addressed. In less than a minute he is through the gate and out on to the road.

He could not have entered by the gate of course. I should have heard him or seen him or both—unless he came before I was out of my room before eight o'clock, and that did not seem very likely. No, he must have come over the fields, and entered the grounds the back way via the orchard. This takes at least half an hour even for a very quick walker. The condition of his shoes bore out the supposition—he had gone through the wet grass. But the point was, why? I was unable at the time to fathom it.

In the afternoon about half past two, just after Audrey had retired for her rest, Marion came out on to the terrace, busied herself there for some minutes. I was standing at the time among the trees just beyond the lawn, so I had a clear view of her. She took up a position in the middle of the terrace, stood straight and still for a second or two then produced from somewhere on her person what looked like a large white handkerchief. Holding it by one corner at arm's length, she shook it as if trying to shake the dust out. After a minute or so of this she went back inside the house. There was in this series of actions something deliberate and also inherently improbable. I suspected immediately that it was a signal. This suspicion was confirmed some five minutes later when the gardener came walking boldly up the drive. He passed by where I was standing and went on, not following the drive round to the front of the house, but taking the path that led along to the outhouses at the back. As soon as I saw him take this path, I felt certain that he was making for the copse and that Marion would shortly follow. I waited a further twelve minutes then I left my place of concealment, and stepped out on to the drive. I went through the house and conservatory and out into the orchard. There was no sign, of course, of either of them. Taking the same route that I had used before I began working my way round to the point of vantage behind the hedge from which I could overlook the copse.

It took me longer this time—twenty-five minutes nearly— and I was not sure for most of the way why I was behaving thus, why I was continuing to keep this pair under surveillance. It was not a desire for personal gratification, I did not expect to see anything much happening, not amid that foliage, nor was there any further advantage to be gained with my sister, in fact repetition might deaden resentment in that quarter. Repeatedly, as I crouched and crept my way along, I asked myself why, why endure such discomforts? What's Hecuba to me? It was not until much later that I finally understood: I had released a certain energy in the world; whatever resulted had to be *contained*. I could not let it get out of hand—signals, assignations, caresses going on all about the place, unregistered, unrecorded; I had to follow them, once again, had to squat behind the hedge, try to make sense of what they, of what we all, were doing.

This time they were not visible, even to the extent of their legs; they had retreated farther into the vegetation, into the very middle of the copse, tunnelling farther and farther from the light, it would seem. So there was nothing to see for quite a long time—only the tops of the bushes, still in the sunshine, the pale trunks of trees, the glint of insects' wings. Then suddenly from the heart of the bushes I heard Marion's voice, a voice richer and more confident than any we had heard her use at home.

'Well, Mr Clever,' she said. 'What colour is it then?' The gardener made some muttered reply and she repeated the question in the same clear, glad voice. 'What colour is it then?' His answer was again inaudible. 'Wrong, that's wrong, you don't really love me,' she said but very happily, as if quite convinced of the contrary. 'Think again,' she said, and at precisely this moment two figures appeared at the crest of the hill leading down to the copse. They seemed to pause briefly, then proceeded steadily downwards. Had they been directly behind the copse I do not think I should have seen them, in spite of the rising ground, because the foliage of the birches would have obstructed my view; but they appeared some way over to the right and then advanced down the field towards the copse diagonally, and so I was able to observe their progress for perhaps two or three minutes. I recognised one of the two figures as the gardener's friend, Cade.

'You should have said, it is the colour of your eyes, the colour of your hair, things like that,' Marion said. 'That's what he said in the story.'

The other man was fair-haired and not so tall. They advanced steadily across the field, not appearing to talk to each other. It was obvious that they were making for the copse and equally obvious that they could not be seen by either Marion or the gardener from within the bushes. I watched them fascinated until they were lost to view behind the copse, hearing at the same time Marion's teasing voice continue: 'What you should have said, only you didn't and it's too late now, is love can be any colour. In this story she asked him that. They were in a restaurant overlooking the Mediterranean Sea. She had been badly let down by an advertising man, before the story proper started and she wouldn't believe anything any of them said. So, she tested him, see? What colour is love? she said to him. You are always going on about it, she said, what colour is it then? And he said, It is the exact identical shade as your eyes.'

He did not reply, perhaps dumbfounded by the ready wit of this fictional person. 'You see?' she said and at that moment there was a low whistle from just beyond the copse.

'What was that? Where are you going?' I heard her say in a different, sharper tone. She said something more, but it was rendered indistinct by a series of muffled crashing sounds from the bushes beyond. I could see nothing. 'Josiah!' I heard the girl cry, in a voice of alarm and entreaty, then again, 'Josiah!' The gardener emerged very quickly from the bushes on the side nearer to me, leapt the rubbish tip, stumbled, slipped to his knees, clawed himself upright again with a rather horrifying haste. He went at a sort of jog-trot along the inside of the hedge, disappeared for some moments, then twenty yards farther down I saw his head and shoulders pushing under the hedge into the open on my side. The crashing sounds had ceased. Marion now uttered a series of sharp cries, on the last of which she seemed to choke. Thereafter she was silent for a while. Josiah had regained his feet. He might easily have seen me, but he stood tensely with his back to the hedge, looking straight before him across the field. And now, quite clearly audible to both the gardener and myself there were sounds of scuffling, a male voice grunting as if at some exertion and a reiterated low whimpering similar to a sound made by an impatient dog. I supposed this last sound was being made by Marion. After listening to it for perhaps two minutes, the gardener craned his head forward, opened his mouth wide and after a brief pause vomited on to the grass before him. He regarded his vomit for some seconds, choked, shuddered, writhed a moment, and vomited again, more copiously. Then he straightened up, wiped his mouth with the back of his hand and began to walk rather unsteadily away, keeping to the line of the hedge.

The memory of that slightly staggering retreat is the last

one that I have of the gardener. I never saw him again. He looked as he receded, with his narrow, elegant back, his stricken gait, immeasurably lonely and without resource. I had the fancy as I watched him go that he had been wounded in a battle and, seeking the dressing station, had lost himself in a landscape that was neutral, quite indifferent to the outcome of the battle and his wound. His body would be found where he fell, far from here—found in foetal elegance, among flowers, by some totally unprepared person. . . .

The whimpering ceased. I heard some muttering then the sound of bodies forcing through the vegetation. They were retiring then. Marion had begun to weep, though not noisily. That quiet weeping of the betrayed and violated girl was difficult to endure. It may seem callous to some, cowardly to others, that I remained there with these fancies, taking no action while undoubtedly violence was being done to Marion. But things happened much more quickly than might appear from this account. Moreover, and more particularly, the copse was not my territory. It belonged, and what happened there belonged, to them. I existed only on the other side of the hedge. How can I explain? There was for me no entrance, no way of exchanging observation for action. So I did nothing but wait until the coast was clear and then, with the utmost circumspection, Marion's weeping still in my ears, begin to withdraw.

Josh ...

IT WAS HERE he said to wait. I know I haven't made no mistake about it. Over against the railing, he said. Just to the left of the Pier Arcade. Your left as you are standing with your back to it. You mean the other side from where the bloke is selling papers? That's right, he said, you wait there. There couldn't be no mistake about that. Why is he late then? I can see the bus-station clock from here and it is getting on for eight. It is ten minutes to. Half past seven, he said. Get an early start, get on the road early, get the long distance trucks. And here we are, nearly eight o'clock. Even if I got it wrong, which side of the Arcade to wait, I would still see him if he come the other side. I mean, it's not as if it was crowded. There's not many people about, this time of day. A few of the locals fishing off the pier, the odd bloke coming over from one of the boarding houses over the way for fags or papers, nobody on the sands at all except this old couple walking beside the sea, right out where the sand is wet. It is going to be a hot day. The sun is clear of the houses already, straight in my eyes when I look that way.

Gone eight, now. *What if Mortimer don't come?* I got no way of finding him. He won't be on the stall, not after what happened, nor at his digs neither. I couldn't go looking for him anyway. I have to get out whether Mortimer comes or not but I dunno where I would go on my own. After what I done to Marion there is no point going anywhere on my own, might as well jump off the pier. I will have to get out though, Marion

will maybe of put the police on to us. I mean, you have to be a
realist, you have to admit there is a possibility. Not that I think
she would of done, myself. Marion is not the girl to go to the
police, not for a thing like that. The coppers asking her, what
happened exactly, what did these men do to you, looking her
over all the time like coppers always do because they can't help
it, much as to say, What were you doing in the bushes anyway?
No, I don't think Marion could stand that.

Besides I know what hurt her most wasn't what Lionel done
to her (it was Lionel that done it, not Mortimer). It was me
leaving her and knowing all the time what was going to happen,
it was when she looked at my face and seen that I knew what
was going to happen. I done a terrible thing to Marion, the
worst thing I ever done. I know that. And when she shouted
after me, shouted my name like, it wasn't to keep them off her
she wanted me to come back. She wasn't thinking about that.
It was to keep her and me together. It was to stop me doing
such a terrible thing. But a course, I could not of stopped then,
not after seeing Lionel. (I didn't know then why Mortimer
brought Lionel, it come as a complete surprise, but I know now,
I have thought it all out, sitting all night in the bus-station
waiting-room. There is two reasons, one behind the other as
you might say.)

It was seeing Lionel with him that made me sick, well I was
feeling a bit sickish before but that was mixed up with excitement like, thinking of Mortimer having Marion and me
watching. Maybe I would of stayed and watched, I dunno.
Thinking about Mortimer doing it with Marion give me a sort
of cramp in the stomach. But the thing I have realised is that
Mortimer does not want anything like that, not personally I
mean. Taking the realist point of view, that is the conclusion I
have come to. Mortimer is not interested in screwing nobody.
He is above it, in my opinion. That is the first reason he brought
Lionel. And the second is, he wanted to show me that it is all
only corporeal, he wanted to drive that message home, so he
brought Lionel for the sake of his organ, to show me it doesn't

have to be someone you like, so long as there is the two organs, that is all you need.

I always felt Mortimer was different. When he started on about the way they walk, in front of Lionel, I got this feeling very strong. And the way he goes on about sexual intercourse and that, but never as if he would want anything to do with it personally. He is more interested in mental things. That's why I got a shock when he brought it up about sharing Marion, it was surprising. Then he brought Lionel with him, that was what made me sick, him bringing Lionel, but when I thought about it after I understood that he wouldn't of been no good on his own. And I think now he only took up with Lionel in the first place for the sake of his organ.

Mortimer done it all for my sake, wanting me to take the realist point a view. He didn't want nothing for himself, he is above it.

Twenty past eight.

She wanted it. I could of had it while we was waiting, she was all for it, nudging with her knee like, but I couldn't of done nothing, I was all keyed up. Then she had to start talking. What is the colour of love? she asked me. Something she'd read about in one of her magazines. Love hasn't got no colour, it is a feeling, I told her, but that was not the right answer. I couldn't hardly follow what she said because I was listening all the time for Mortimer. Some bloke in a story going on about the colour of love.

Her face when I got up was not surprised. That was after the whistle. I didn't hear them coming, first thing I heard was the whistle. She didn't look surprised, particularly, not at the whistle or me getting up. I dunno what she thought, maybe she thought I was going to relieve myself. Then the sound of them crashing through the bushes, it was a lot of noise for only one, frightening, she was asking me something but I couldn't hear, then Mortimer come through and Lionel behind him. They both looked dead serious. Mortimer said something to me but I couldn't hear nothing, dunno why, everything went quiet all round me and I couldn't hear nothing till I heard her shouting after me, shouting my name. All before that was quiet, her starting to get up and them moving towards her and me getting out of it, up the bank. Soon as I started hearing things again I knew I was going to be sick. I will never forget her face when she knew and I will never forget her voice when she shouted after me.

I know there is nothing wrong with the way she walks. I knew it all along.

Mortimer and me done a terrible thing to Marion. Mortimer and me done it together. Lionel don't count. Anyone with a male member would of done as well as Lionel, he is not in it at all, it is just me and Mortimer. Doing something like that brings you close together with a person. That is why he has got to come. If Mortimer don't come, there will be no point to it, we will of done that terrible thing for nothing.

Half past eight. Please Mortimer, you got to come. Please God let Mortimer come. Please God. . . .

That is him. I see him right at the end of the promenade, alone on the empty pavement, carrying his suitcase. No one else walks like that, holding himself straight up. Yes it is him, in his navy-blue suit. (I knew all along he would come, a course —Mortimer never breaks his word.) He is still on the other side, walking towards me, getting nearer, but now I don't see him so well, because of the sun, the sun is behind him and it is shining straight into my eyes. Mortimer starts crossing the road and it is like he is coming out of the sun, I can't look at him, the sun hurts my eyes, brings tears to my eyes. I close my eyes for a second and then he is beside me and I see that he is smiling. Sorry Josiah, he says, I was unavoidably retarded (his own words), and I know it is really him and we are going off on the road together. We will always be together now.

Simon ...

WHAT WAS STRANGE indeed was the silence that ensued. The gardener did not reappear, of course. Audrey kept to her room. Marion continued to minister to us both with a depressed, but not at all resentful air. She was busy during this time, however, with her own affairs, letters must have been written and received because on the ninth day following her misadventure in the copse she announced that she was leaving us. This announcement of hers in fact was the first breaking of the silence.

There was a second, more violent one, two days after her departure.

Looking already not quite the same person, as though the imminence of that departure had effected a definite though inexpressible change in her, in a chocolate-brown suit that I thought I recognised as having once belonged to Audrey, she stood waiting in the hall, her single suitcase strapped and ready at the foot of the grandfather clock, which has been sadly disordered since Howard's death, and now, as I was crossing the hall towards her, at eighteen minutes to eleven, chimed solemnly five times. While she waited there for her taxi I spoke to her and she spoke to me and between us we put an end to the silence that had been lying over the house.

'You knew all along, didn't you?' she said to me. I was still crossing the hall when she said this, intent on wishing her *bon voyage* and handing over a gift I had bought for her the day before, a pair of circular earrings fashioned in copper, which I thought would be acceptable. I had the sequence of words and actions involved in all this carefully worked out, but her remarking that I had known all along took the wind out of my sails completely. I handed over the little black box in silence—nodding and smiling of course, as I always do in interim periods.

She looked at them for a moment in their box, then she took them out and put them on. They did not really suit her very well, I thought. She was going to Durham to stay with some relative of her mother's. 'Thank you very much,' she said now. 'They're lovely.'

I was most perturbed to see that tears had come into her eyes. 'Don't cry,' I said, and this completely unpremeditated injunction released an emotion in myself which must have been lurking there in wait for just such a set of circumstances. In her white face, the painful prominence of her teeth, the tears in her eyes, I saw the bereaved child who had come to us seven years before, departing as she had arrived, in grief and loneliness; and my own eyes moistened as I accused myself of having regarded her merely as a figure in a pattern, never a single suffering person.

The tendency so to regard everyone, cultivated early and now quite habitual, had cost me the power of a genuinely sympathetic response—as though I had been applying over the years a sort of slow but insatiable leech to my affective faculties. Too late now of course. There was no way, no way unattended by irony or deliberate self-distancing, of conveying to Marion my feeling of sorrow. I tried, however. I stopped nodding and smiling. I even raised my hand and touched Marion on the cheek, actually touched with my finger tips the surface of her face, a gesture I could hardly believe I was making. 'Don't cry,' I repeated. 'He really isn't worth it.'

This, without intention on my part, was the right thing to say because it stiffened Marion immediately. The tears proceeded no farther. 'You mustn't say that,' she said, and there was authority in her voice. 'He was led astray. He is easily led. He hero-worshipped that Cade.'

'Well I suppose he did, er, does,' I said. 'All the same—'

'No,' she said. 'It is being easily led that is his trouble. He won't ever come back here. But he knows where to find me. If he ever wants to find me he will know where I am. . . .'

It seemed to me now that Marion had begun to speak in an unnatural way like one of those heroines in her *True Romances* and I was relieved to hear the approaching taxi.

'Well, I'll be going,' she said. She had made a distinct recovery during our conversation. The affirmation of Josiah's worth had cheered her, apparently; or perhaps the assurance that he knew where she was to be found. At any rate she departed holding her head up and smiling. I carried her suitcase to the taxi.

After Marion left, silence settled over the house again. Silence and dust. Audrey remained in her room, making foraging trips to the kitchen when she thought I would not be about, for cream crackers, tea, things of that sort. I myself relied chiefly on tinned soups during this period. It was an uncomfortable time for us both. I suffered from feelings of lassitude and depression, perhaps in reaction to the strain of the previous weeks, and spent most of the time in my room.

Then at a few minutes after nine, on the evening of the second day following Marion's departure, the silence was again broken, but this time more dramatically. I had just consumed a tin of mushroom soup and was in my room, looking through some old copies of *Nova* for stocking advertisements to cut out and stick in my scrap-book. (These pictures of women in the act of putting on stockings I find very stimulating, the deliberateness and at the same time carelessness of the exposure.) Suddenly, I heard a very peculiar sound from Audrey's room, with a bubbling, almost gargling quality in it. I sat for some seconds, but the sound was not repeated. It was rather difficult to know what to do. I did not think that I could have been mistaken, but I was naturally reluctant to intrude on Audrey's privacy. I listened intently. There was no sound at all. Neither from inside nor outside the house. This silence, in fact, now that I had begun particularly to register it, was oppressive and rapidly grew more so. It seemed to me like the silence that hangs over abandoned places.

I rose and laid my *Nova* carefully aside. A last look down at the open page, that dreaming face, those heedless thighs. Then I left my room and went along the passage. I listened at Audrey's door but could hear nothing. I tapped lightly on the door. There was no response. I tapped more loudly. 'Are you all right, Audrey?' I called. There was some reply, I thought but very faint, I could not distinguish it. Perhaps she was ill. I turned the handle. The door was not locked. I half opened it and put my head into the room. 'Are you all right?' I said. Audrey was sitting up in bed, bolt upright, with the sheet drawn up to her chin in what struck me at first as a rather histrionic spasm of modesty. She had obviously been watching the door intently. Now she stared at me in a curiously wide-eyed, watchful way, as though she were expecting me to behave outrageously.

'Is everything all right?' I said again. 'I thought I heard you calling out.'

'Go away,' Audrey said, or whimpered rather, and I should probably have obeyed despite the strangeness of her manner, had I not seen the blood. An irregular patch of it on the sheet just below Audrey's chin. At that distance it was merely a dark stain but I identified it immediately as blood, my mind made an intuitive leap. 'That is blood,' I said, and I advanced into the room. The patch was now much bigger, and spreading rapidly, soaking through the sheet below Audrey's face. Her wide-eyed expression did not change, but when I put out my hand towards the sheet, she opened her mouth and screamed. I took the sheet and drew it away from her. There was blood everywhere. The front of Audrey's flannel dressing gown was covered with blood and all the left side of her neck and shoulder. There were little puddles of blood in the folds of the lower sheet.

The knife was not found till much later. It was the breadknife she had used. She had sat there and sawed through the left side of her neck. Then she called out, just once. If it had not been for that she would almost certainly have bled to death; or so the doctor said. She had not been able to repress it, sensing how terribly she had damaged herself. At any rate, by the time I entered, her resolve had hardened again; she had genuinely wanted me to go away, leave her alone to die. I will not readily forget how her attempt to hide this ebbing of her blood resembled at the time a sort of exaggerated modesty, nor how she screamed when I forced the sheet from her, when she knew her wound was about to be detected. . . .

Audrey has always anticipated everything. It does not strike me as surprising that she should anticipate her end. What I do find difficult to understand is the ferocity of the means employed, the self-mutilation. She has never discussed her reasons with me nor indeed made any but the obliquest references to the episode. I shall never know for certain why she chose to hack at herself with a breadknife.

I shall never know either, probably, what Mr Cade said to her the day I met him in the grounds with wet shoes. I think his main object that day had been to reconnoitre the copse, get the lie of the land so to speak. But it is my belief that he took the opportunity of telling Audrey something that destroyed her pleasure in the horse. Perhaps he told her that it had been intended in the first place for him. . . .

At any rate Audrey recovered. But owing to the damage to the tendons of the neck on one side she is now obliged to keep her head tilted at an angle about thirty degrees to the vertical. This gives people the impression that she is listening intently for some very faint sound, just as when I came upon her in the drive that day calling Josiah's name and listening with her head cocked for an answer that never came. . . .

She would not leave the house at first. I had everything to do, everything. (It was during this period that I encountered Major Donaldson at the Post Office, and made an enemy of him.) Little by little, however, she has regained confidence, though still very conscious of her deformity of course. I take her for walks, the devoted brother. No question now of my leaving. We have engaged a maid, more robust than poor Marion and much less given to reading. One day last week, when we were walking down the High Street, happening to glance behind me, I caught some small boys imitating my sister's gait, mincing along the pavement with their heads cocked. One of them was that round-headed boy whom Audrey had permitted to wander in the grounds. He showed no sign of recognition.

These October days are excellent for digging. I am hoping to reach the front hedge by spring. Then, when the warm weather comes, I shall be able to watch the careless cycling girls.